HIS WILD IRISH ROSE

DE CLARE LEGACY

STACEY REYNOLDS

HIS WILD IRISH ROSE ©

COPYRIGHT BY STACEY REYNOLDS

OTHER WORKS BY STACEY
REYNOLDS

Raven of the Sea: An O'Brien Tale
A Lantern in the Dark:An O'Brien Tale
Shadow Guardian: An O'Brien Tale
River Angels: An O'Brien Tale
The Wishing Bridge
Fio: An O'Brien Novella

PROLOGUE

*R*ose Tierney drove within eyeshot of London, expecting a dramatic change of scenery. England... The great forbidden territory. Although her father was born in Blackpool, he'd lived in London for over twenty years. She'd spent the bulk of her life in a small town just north of Belfast and hadn't set foot in London since she was a small child. She had a modest home that was safe and clean but filled to bursting with things unsaid. Secrets were hanging from the eaves and clinging to the windows, not willing to let the full light of the sun shine on her small family. Her grandmother and her little brother were all she had in the world. Well, not technically, hence the trip to London. Her grandmother falsely thought she was doing work-study in Italy for four weeks. She'd taken this trip because she was running out of time.

She looked ahead, the wind whipping against her helmet as she exited the M1 at Brent Cross, and she thought that she should have seen demons flying overhead. Armed snipers ready to attack. It was silly, of course. She was an educated woman. But after almost twenty years of absence, the imagi-

1

nation tended to take over. Twenty years ago she'd been a small child and her brother Kieran had been a baby. But fear was a powerful thing, especially in regular, consistent doses. Especially when it was spoon fed to a child.

She'd been six years old when her mother had died. Six years old when her father had called her maternal grandmother and dropped them off in Northern Ireland. They never saw him again. The last thing he said to her was that there were devils over the water. Devils lived in London. He assured her that it was better this way. He kissed her on the cheek and held her in his big, tattooed arms. Her father always smelled like leather and the pub, but she'd never minded because he also smelled like the wind. She could still see him, pulling into the apartment parking lot at all hours of the day and night, a helmet and tattered jeans. A leather vest with some sort of patches on it.

It was hard to recall the details, but the smells she remembered. Her mother smelled like body lotion and coffee. The rest was blank. She'd died right before Rose's father shipped them off to Ireland. Six years old and she remembered almost nothing. Like someone had taken an eraser to her memories. Stolen her mother from her. She looked through photos, tried hypnosis, but nothing worked. Smells, however, were hard to erase. The response was more visceral.

Rose pushed those thoughts aside. Her mother wasn't here, but she'd bet her last quid that her father was still in London. He'd be older now, but people never really changed that much. He hadn't been that hard to find, once she put her mind to it. The desperate search for her father had become necessary, and quite possibly life and death. She'd begun on the internet, and the pieces had started to fall into place. So she'd rung him up on her mobile, and miraculously, he'd answered. Some hovel on the east end, from the looks of the internet maps. The briefest phone call of her life, or at least it seemed that way. He'd said two sentences for a start. *Never call me again. It isn't safe.*

Typical cryptic shite. *I don't care, Da. It's Kieran. I am not being dramatic when I say that his life depends on you getting your ass to Belfast and being a feckin' father for once in your bloody life!* The pause was long, but he didn't hang up. *I will contact you, not the other way around. Do ye hear, girl? You wait for my call.* She'd leaned into the phone like he was directly in front of her. *I don't care if you have to put floaties on that bike and row over the Irish Sea. You come, or I come for you.*

The call ended, and she'd waited three days. When she called back, the phone was disconnected. So she was going to find that son-of-a-bitch the old fashioned way. She was going to hit the streets of East London and track him down.

JACKSON DE CLARE eased on the leather biker jacket as he looked over the Thames River from the expansive windows of his latest acquisition. He'd lived in many parts of London, never settling for long. This new penthouse in Battersea was by far his most unspoiled view. When word of the power-house restoration had hit his radar, he'd gone to the developer that afternoon and put down a hefty deposit. Now he owned 3500 square feet of riverfront, ultra-modern living.

He ran his hand over the soft leather. A perfect fit. But then again, he'd always been comparable in size to his brother, despite their different coloring. But where he was accustomed to fine tailoring from an exclusive Japanese tailor, Louie had been more at home in concert t-shirts and denim. Probably because it irritated their mother. Good boys from wealthy families didn't wear Levis to dinner.

Not that it mattered now. His mother was as clueless as

always, living in Chelsea and finding her next event to chair. His father was eight years in his grave, and now Louie was gone. The only bright light in their otherwise dismal family dynamic was his sister Amelia. She was away at university. She was a dance major, and tough as nails. The first time he'd gotten a gander at her feet following a long week of rehearsals, he'd almost rushed her to the doctor. Dancing was a hard way to spend your days. She trained relentlessly, watched every bite that went in her mouth, and didn't have time for friends or the usual debauchery that went on in those early college years. He still remembered driving to her dormitory, sitting her down, and telling her about their brother.

The pain washed through him anew, and he felt the leather stretch across his biceps as he clenched his fists. Good boys from wealthy families weren't supposed to die in some piss-soaked alley in East Ham. And some men were boys until the day they died. His brother had been twenty-eight. Old enough to have his act together, to have started a career, maybe even acquired a wife. Instead, he'd pursued the next thrill-seeking adventure by getting a motorcycle. Not a Ducati or a BMW like other men they knew, or even a Triumph like he'd had in his twenties. No, Louie had gone for one of those enormous American bikes. It would be Harley Davidson or nothing. The decline had been slow. Most men with motorcycles did rides out in the country, took it up the coast, or commuted for better parking and petrol prices. Not Louie. He'd gone all in, as he usually did. The fervor of a new convert. Leather clad, tattooed, morally unsound comrades to ride through the worst parts of London, living fast and looking for trouble.

The real problems had come when he'd begun hanging on the fringes of one of the more notorious motorcycle clubs. Always drawn to the element of danger, it had been irresistible. And the men knew their trade. The women as well. They smelled the old money and discontent rolling off of his brother. The drugs, in hindsight, had been inevitable. As devastated as their mother had been, she'd just shaken her head and commented on her failure as a mother. Then she'd buried herself in another committee and refused to talk about him.

Christ, if she only knew that both her sons had broken with convention. When Jack had broached the subject of law enforcement as a potential career eight years ago, she'd almost had a stroke. Apparently nice boys from wealthy families didn't dirty their hands with public service either, unless it was in the parliament. So, she thought he was an expert in international finance. Sure, he'd finished business school. But then he'd been recruited into MI5, Great Britain's national law enforcement agency, and never looked back. His mother hadn't known and still didn't. Neither had his brother. They'd never understood him. They were both as self-centered as the other, just in different ways. His father had understood him. Jackson, Sr. had been a pilot in the Royal Navy. With all his money and influence, he'd graduated from Oxford and done a commitment in the military. Jackson Sr.'s own father had fought the Nazis when he was little more than a boy, and he felt that every man worth his salt should serve his country. He'd tried to instill that in both his sons. It hadn't stuck with Louie.

Jack's work with MI5 was covert and usually restricted to working cases in the fast-paced and polished world of corporate crime. That was until his brother had overdosed beside his motorcycle, his back leaned up against a rubbish bin. This was personal. The Sons of the Fallen motorcycle club were a scourge on London, and they were spreading. There were chapters popping up all over the UK. They were responsible for a huge heroin influx into the cities, a steady supplying pouring in from Asia. The London chapter president, Bobby Clyde, may as well have put a bullet in his brother's head. The dose he'd been given from Bobby's dealer was laced with fentanyl and would have been fatal for a five hundred pound sumo wrestler. But what was a little miscalculation on dosage when income was at stake?

Jack's superiors had forbidden him to touch the ongoing investigation of the gang's activity until he'd threatened to walk. He was deep in the white collar crime world, but he would quit that moment if they didn't let him step back from that work and help on this case. It's not like he did it for the money. He could afford to never work again. So they'd acquiesced, and his transition had begun. He stopped shaving and cutting his hair, started polishing up on his riding. He'd owned his own motorcycle several years ago, and it all came back to him with stunning ease. He got a custom paint job on his brother's bike and had begun slowly infiltrating the world of hardcore bikers. Maybe he'd put Bobby Clyde in prison for the rest of his life, but if he couldn't, he'd put him in the ground.

CHAPTER 1

*R*ose woke to the sound of traffic. She groaned as she rolled over in her sleeping bag. She eyed the lantern through the small amount of light she had. She'd arranged a small garage rental in Newham. It was smelly and small. It was inconceivable that someone could fit a car in this tiny space. She hadn't had the funds for a hotel or even a cheap AirBnB, and she had no plans to stay long. She'd secured the garage and had the owner's permission to camp inside it with her bike, something she couldn't afford to have stolen. She helped support her family, and this bike was way cheaper than a car. Horrible in the rain, which happened often in Ireland, but it got her around and was easy to park. She didn't feel the lack of a car was a failure. Only American telly showed twenty-four-year-olds with hot cars or kick ass pickup trucks. They were practically still in nappies when they started driving.

The housing was another matter. Her father sent money to her grandmother. She knew this. But it wasn't much, and her grandmother had a mortgage note to pay, food to buy, and other expenses. The only reason Rose had been able to send Kieran to the small Catholic school she'd attended was because she worked full time and then some. Now she was paying for some online classes for him because he needed a flexible schedule.

She'd taken a few classes at a time at the local college, but the money was tight. She'd been trying to become a nurse for six years, and she finally finished her coursework last month. The hospital where she'd done her residency had positions opening at the first of the year, and she was at the top of their list. No more singing in pubs or waiting tables for money. She'd be a nurse.

She didn't have those wages coming in yet, however. Hence the campsite in some shitty garage in a dodgy part of London. The tipsy house was also a dump, and the owner didn't have a car, so this situation was all she could hope for as long as she was in London. A totally illegal arrangement, but there you have it. There was a 24-hour Spar market less than a block away if she needed a midnight run to the water closet or a snack, but she needed a regular shower which she'd negotiated as part of the arrangement. Shower access every other day for fifteen minutes.

By the looks of the outside, she was horrified to think about the condition of the shower. Her home was humble, but it was clean and well maintained. She quickly washed her face with the rinsing bowl she'd set up with a cheap plastic bowl and bottled water. She'd never been the sort to primp. She washed her face with soap and water, brushed her teeth, and ran a wet brush through her long hair. Then she dressed in her jeans, t-shirt, and leather jacket.

It was early autumn, so the night hadn't been too cold with the bedroll and old sleeping bag. She used a hoodie for a pillow. Sliding her boots on, she punched in the coordinates for the neighborhood club that was owned by a Fallen member. She was hoping like hell she'd just walk in and her da would be sitting at the bar, but she was winging it at this point. If she had to stay longer, she'd ask about a job. A non-whoring, non-drug dealing job. She'd read enough about the criminal activity of this motorcycle club that mistaking her for an addict or whore might be a realistic risk she was taking by walking through the door. *Courage. Your brother doesn't have time for cowards.*

* * *

JACK WALKED into the dive bar in East Ham where the Sons of the Fallen had their meetings and various forms of club recreation. Women, liquor, drugs, and a good fist fight every now and again. The newest prospect, Sammy, was sweeping a pile of broken glass into a dustpan. "Morning Jack. You're in early."

"Sammy, it's one o'clock. How late did you sleep?" The young man's smile was devilish.

"The more important question would be, why was I up so late?"

"Well, I hope she was worth it. Is it too early for a pint of bitter?" Jack had lived in London his whole life. And, although his family was affluent, his mates from school had taught him a thing or two about blending in. This skill had been polished during his training with MI5. Picking up on the regional accents was crucial. He could tell the difference between someone from Cornwall and Cardiff; Blackpool and Liverpool; Glasgow and the Highlands. There were finer nuances that helped him gather intel and adopt the local cadence when he was trying to blend in. He knew how to shed the private school diction and Earl of Shittingtom accent he'd grown up with.

"Oh, she was worth it. Plump thighs and a small mouth. Just my type," Sammy said with a grin. *Jesus*, Jack thought as

9

he shook his head. Young and stupid just like his brother. Hopefully, he'd worn a condom. These club members passed girls around like a shared bag of crisps. Jack had never understood it. He had an extremely healthy sex drive even though he was thirty, but he didn't share. And he didn't take sloppy seconds...or sloppy twelfths in this case. If he had a regular lay, he made it clear that he was the only quill being dipped in the inkwell for the time they spent together. Prospects, sadly, were at the bottom of the list. The girls that whored in the club liked the prospects. They were usually younger and enthusiastic. Better than the grey-bearded, fat asses that got seniority points for the fuck pool. He quelled the urge to shiver.

He looked up as the club president and bar owner walked in. Sharp as a tack, he seemed impervious to hangovers. He partied with his boys to a degree, but he was the head dick-head in charge. The brains of the operation, although he wasn't lacking in the brawn. Shaved head, silver goatee, tall and broad-shouldered, he looked like pure menace. He was a Belfast import, ties to the IRA. But he relocated early on with the M.C. for unknown reasons. He was a private man, and he was deadly. MI5 had never been able to make any charges stick. He covered his ass with a trail of minions that did his dirty work. Shrewd blue eyes narrowed on him. "Jackknife," he nodded. That was it. No *hello how are ye* out of this guy. Then the door dinged and he put a hand up to the prospect. "I'll get it. Keep sweeping and then clean the toilets. That's what you get for jumping the line in front of your betters."

"Yes, sir," Sammy said solemnly, then he gave Jack a wink. She really must have been worth it.

As Jack looked up from his pint of bitter, his breath cut short. Through the doorway walked an absolutely stunning woman. More like a girl. She looked about nineteen. Auburn hair, perfect skin, long legs, and a small, fitted Triumph t-shirt. Pretty ballsy considering the Harley vibe in this club. She had her ratty leather jacket in her hand. She met his eyes and he almost swooned on his bar stool. She didn't have the typical blue or green eyes of her coloring, nor the spicy ginger colored eyes that were the alternative for a redhead. She had pools of chocolate. Dark and rich and so innocent, he felt like throwing her over his shoulder and running her right back out that front door.

He looked at Bobby, a.k.a. Luce, short for Lucifer, the most notorious fallen angel. Luce was not unaffected. In fact, it was the most emotion he'd ever seen on his face. Want and pain mixed with a shot of pure lust that he was trying like hell to control. His jaw was tight as he watched the young woman like a predator. *Interesting.* He led her to a booth, then went to the bar to get her what looked like a club soda.

Luckily the bar didn't draw a crowd until the partiers rolled out of bed. He was able to hear most of what sounded like an interview.

ROSE LOOKED across the table at what she could only describe as Satan himself. Ice blue eyes, lined face, although she'd put him close to her father's age, which was probably around fifty. He was tall and strong and moved like a predator. If she'd been into older men, he was admittedly a bit on the dangerously sexy side. But she'd let her daddy issues go a long time ago. Definitely not her type. He'd introduced himself as simply Luce. No last name, and she doubted it was his given name. Familiarity niggled at her mind, but she couldn't place him.

"So, you're from the island? Whereabouts?" His voice was harsh and commanding as if she didn't have any choice but to answer. She detected some Irish in the tones, which was a surprise. She'd assumed that the head of the London chapter would be English.

"Ballyclare in Antrim."

"Aye, I know it. So, what's your business?"

"I was…" She thought about it. It was not time to tip her hand. She needed to find her dad, and she didn't want to spook him or expose herself just yet. She had no idea what his standing was with the club. If someone had a grudge, she'd end up in a dumpster. "I was looking for work." Luce didn't seem like a man who was surprised very often, but his brows twitched. Then he smiled.

"Are ye now? Well, we've only got a few positions for women that look like you, so what is your skill set? Blowjobs or pharmaceuticals?"

Dread washed over her, even though she'd expected this. Her Catholic school upbringing was at war with her current predicament. She decided to play it hard. She stood abruptly, the crappy table wobbling as she started to exit the booth. "This was a mistake. I'll try another countryman. You've been in London too long, Mr. Luce."

He snatched her arm and flipped it to expose the pale skin of her forearm. "No tattoos. Pretty uncommon in this neck of the woods. No track marks either."

She leaned in. "Because no one marks me, and I don't mess with that shit. I need a job. I like the bikes. I'm no whore, so take your hand off me before you pull back a stump."

Then he did something that surprised the hell out of her. He laughed. He cracked off a loud laugh. Then he looked at Sammy. "Pay attention, lad. Irish lasses are the only ones worth the effort." He let her arm go. "Sit." It wasn't a request.

She tightened her jaw, and she knew what her face looked like. She wanted to slap him senseless, which seemed to amuse him. His eyes sparkled with mirth. It had been a risk to go nose to nose with him, and she wasn't going to push her luck by demanding an apology.

She cleared her throat. "I have waitress and bartending experience, and I'm a musician. I don't suppose you're too worried about live music. This doesn't seem to be the traditional session sort of pub. I can pour drinks, smile, even bat my eyelashes and wiggle my ass. That ass, however, is not for sale. If your patrons have a mind for rape, I will put a stake in their heart or die trying. Are you able to control them?"

He cocked his head at her gall. "My boys don't wipe unless I declare it shit. But tell me this. Why in the hell would I hire you when I can get a whore to do the same job and get my cock stroked at the end of the night?"

"Because druggy whores usually steal. If they don't steal, they get high and run their mouths. And if they've been on their feet all night waiting tables, they're less likely to give you a good rub." His grin infuriated her. "I'll work every night. I want cash. Ten pounds an hour plus any tips these cheap English bastards are willing to give."

Something was so off, Jack could actually smell it. This girl did not scream barfly. When Luce had grabbed her, Jack had one foot on the ground ready to intervene. He was bordering on losing his bloody mind, actually. That little Irish honey needed to get the hell out of here. But she'd stood her own, and maybe it was the Irish connection, or maybe it was one alpha giving grudging respect to another. Not only had he backed off with the crude, brutish behavior, but the little shit had actually negotiated a job from him. It didn't sit right, though. If he didn't know better, he'd wonder if she was another copper working undercover. But that was impossible. There was a ban from the highest level that ensured there weren't too many cooks in the kitchen when it came to investigating the Sons of the Fallen.

One of the other girls came out of the office. She looked

like she'd had a rough night. Luce stood, nodding to the girl. "Show her the kitchen and the bar area and how to work the register. She'll work until half ten." He began walking away when he stopped. "What's your name, lass?"

"Rose." She offered nothing else. He narrowed his eyes, taking in her features.

"How did you find my club, Rose? We don't exactly advertise."

"My cousin rides. He's a mate of one of your club members. When I told him I needed work, he sent me here," she answered.

"And who might that club member be?"

"Mick Tierney. Is he around?"

Luce froze for a brief moment, then stared at her like he was memorizing every inch of her face. "Mick is busy."

CHAPTER 2

$\mathcal{C}$andice finished showing Rose how to work the old register. No computerized touch pads here. She was a nice enough lady, even though she smelled like stale beer, smoke, and male cologne, which cleared up what her side job must be after hours. She turned to her only customer, ready to ask him if he needed another pint, and she stopped dead at the sight of him. Holy shit. He was ridiculously handsome. Shaggy brown hair in his eyes, probably a week's worth of beard growth, and a perfect mouth. His eyes were deep blue, like a stormy sea. Perfect, thick, shapely brows, and a sculpted jawline. He was out of place in this ugly environment, he was so good looking. His leathers didn't have the patches of the Sons of the Fallen, so he was either on the fringes, or he was just an unlikely walk-in customer.

"Can I pull you another pint? Bitter, is it?" His eyes met hers. He didn't give her an overtly sexual look, but his eyes flared and she felt her heart skip.

"You can, and thank you." Hmm, polite too. She started pouring and glanced at him, hoping a side glance might reveal some flaws. Nope. She slid the pint in front of him and he took it, thanking her again.

"You don't seem the sort to hang out in a biker bar, despite the leather," she said, narrowing her eyes on his face.

"I might say the same thing about you, Rose. It was Rose, wasn't it?" She nodded, whether to concede the point or verify her name, he didn't know. He also noticed a blush forming on her cheeks like she wasn't used to flirting. Had they been flirting? Yes, a sweet, pink blush on the apples of her cheeks. Jesus, she really needed to get out of here.

It was interesting, though, to see the effect she had on Luce. He didn't seem the sort to get sappy over a female. Who was this woman, and who the hell was Mick Tierney? He needed to call Katherine, their in-house, human computer that they'd all be lost without, and have her dig into the name. If it came up a dead-end, he wanted this girl out of here. He didn't want her anywhere near the blast radius when Luce got what was coming to him. Not to mention the area was dodgy as hell. East Ham, downwind from the sewage plant, was not what you'd call a tourist area. It had a lot of industry, however. Industry and warehouses and a city airport. Access to the river. So, for someone in the trade of trafficking prostitutes and selling drugs or guns or both, the area was ideal.

He looked at the unlikely barkeep and suddenly felt very old. In his younger years, he'd be in her britches or die trying within the quarter hour. Now he just wanted to protect her. His pedigree background and white collar investigations hadn't prepared him for what he'd seen in the last two weeks. Women used and disposed of like rubbish. Addicts and adrenalin junkies circling for some action. He hated to think of his brother here, and if he dwelled on that too long, he'd kick Luce's door open and choke him out with his own leather belt.

"Deep thoughts. Are you going to be trouble?" Her voice was soft. So soft that only he would have heard the warning. He looked at her beautiful, soft, doe eyes and his whole body warmed.

"Sorry, I'm a little off today." He pushed the untouched pint away. "This is probably a bad idea. See if Sammy wants it." Then he slid a ten-pound note toward her. "Good luck with the new job, Rose. And stay sharp. This isn't Ballyclare. These men play for keeps."

She nodded. "Ditto."

He left the bar, taking note of the little Triumph parked by the door. It looked out of place next to the full-size Harleys and other hunks of metal. He also noticed it was in rough shape. The tires needed replacing, for starters. The tread was almost gone. He looked above him at the hovering rain clouds. It was supposed to start raining about an hour or two before she was done with work. How the hell was she going to ride that thing in the dark while it was raining? He shook himself and mumbled, "Not your problem, Jack. Keep walking."

* * *

ROSE WAS EXHAUSTED as she handed over the bar towel to her co-worker. The men watched Candice like wolves who were ready to feast. They stole glances at her as well, but nothing out of line. She wondered if it was due to the modest attire and lack of flash, or if Luce had stayed true to his word and forbade them to advance on her. Either way, she was glad for it. She had close to no experience with men, and these weren't the type to cut your teeth on. That other one, though. The one who'd been here during her interview and wisely left early. He was another story. As if summoning him from a dream, he was in the doorway. A big bastard, he was well

17

over six feet with broad shoulders and thick, muscled arms and thighs. She exhaled audibly and Candice turned around.

She laughed, "Yes, he's a looker to be sure. All the girls have been after him, but he's not interested." Then she watched as his eyes narrowed on Rose. Candice smiled conspiratorially. "Then again, maybe we wasn't his type." Her thick, cockney accent gave away her working-class, London roots.

Rose turned away, "Men like that don't have types. They have followers. I'll pass." Then she spun around to come from behind the bar and walked straight into Luce. A wall of leather and steel. He grabbed her elbows to steady her, and his blue eyes glowed. "Easy, love. Don't get distracted." Then he switched his gaze to pretty boy. "Jackknife. Good to see you again, mate. Have Candice get you a drink...and anything else you might be looking for." Then he turned back to Rose. She eased out of his hands, blushing under his intense attention.

"Sorry, I was just coming to see you. I'm done for the night." She put her chin up, meeting his eyes.

"Ye did well, lass. Let's go into my office and settle up."

When he closed the door to the office, he sat at his desk, rifled in a drawer, and then handed her a wad of cash. "It's raining. Do you need me to arrange a ride?"

She shook her head. "I'm Irish, Luce. My blood is half rainwater. I'll do. It's just a bit of mist."

He gave a deep, husky laugh. "I suppose it is. How is my fair island? It's been a long time since I called it home."

"Belfast is...still Belfast. They're still fighting. It's just over football instead of religion. It's a bit fast for my taste. Bally-clare is green. Green and small."

"Then why come here?"

"Same reason you did, I suppose. Looking for something else." He leaned back in his chair, his eyes speculative. Before he pried anymore, she said, "Thank you for staying true to our agreement. The men didn't...expect anything. They behaved themselves."

He smiled, and it was predatory. "Aye, well they're rough with their manners, but they follow orders. They didn't like it. They're used to taking what they want."

"And what about you? Do you just take what you want?" she asked, head cocked speculatively.

He shook his head from side to side, slowly, his eyes intense. "No, lass. I make it so that what I want comes to me."

Jack watched the door to Luce's office nervously. The barmaid leaned in. "Don't worry. He won't hurt her. He's not the sort to force a woman." As if on cue, Rose walked out of the office and he watched as Luce's eyes stalked her from the doorway. Fuck, he hated this. He needed to focus. As the spell was broken by her departure, Luce waved a hand. "Candice! Get this lad another drink."

* * *

JACK STIRRED in his bed and groaned. He was bloody hungover, and his head was pounding. He really wasn't cut out for this shit. Last night had been rough. Women with their hands all over him, trying to entice him into a purchase. The offer of a bit of free weed, which he'd declined. They were a suspicious bunch, and he could tell that they'd been testing him. So in the name of camaraderie, he'd cut loose more than he normally did. Shots of tequila off of some woman's tits, for a start. Then twenty-five swats on a woman's leather-clad ass because she'd sworn it was her birthday and laid herself over his lap. If she was twenty-five, then he was the Prince of Wales, but he'd given her what she wanted, to the cheers of the brothers and other patrons.

Jesus. How did they do it every night? He'd barely gotten

free of the place before the threesomes had started. They were like fucking animals. They lived fast and hard, and in some twisted way, he understood why his brother had been drawn to it. He'd always been looking for new ways to shed the starchiness of their proper upbringing. Hadn't Jack done the same, albeit in a more productive direction? His phone started buzzing and he grabbed it off the bureau. "Good morning, Katherine."

"So formal, even hungover. I cannot fathom how you pass yourself off as a biker, Jackson."

"Well, last night it involved copious amounts of cheap tequila."

"That would explain your condition," she said, and he could hear the grin.

He looked down at himself, wondering if they had a camera in his new flat. Not likely, but given the fact that he was in a complete state of undress with a raging erection, he decided to pull the blanket over himself. "You have news, I'm assuming."

"Yes, it's regarding Mick Tierney. I think you should come into the office. This is going to involve more than a phone call." He sat up abruptly. As if reading his mind, she said, "No, not now. Just get dressed, take some tablets, and come to the Cambridge office, out of town. There's a ticket on the 12:15 waiting at the train station."

He ended the call and thought about the woman at the bar, again. *Rose.* She had an alluring, understated beauty that had to do with ivory skin, silky auburn hair, and a perfect, pink mouth. She had intelligent, soulful eyes. It didn't match up with someone who'd seek out a barmaid position in a biker bar. She wasn't tall, but she had long legs, round hips that spread from a smooth waist. His erection kicked as if to weigh in on the matter. Not a good sign.

* * *

Rose dressed quickly after her shower. It had taken her a bit of time because she'd had to clean it first. These really were the worst landlords, but at eight pounds a night she had her plot of shelter to house both herself and her bike. She thought about what Luce had said last night. She offered to take the closing shift tonight, but he'd declined. He wanted her gone by eleven, which was curious. His response to her father's name had been strange as well. Maybe her father came in after hours? She needed to be there later than half ten. There was no good place to hide and watch the front door, and there was the back entrance to consider.

She wiped the fog off of the mirror and brushed her teeth. She wasn't worried about time. This cruddy WC was "the guest bath". No one would be tapping their foot, waiting for the shower to be free. Then she braided her hair. She didn't have many clothes with her, so she opted for a blush colored peasant top. It hardly screamed biker chick, but it was clean. She'd washed her knickers and t-shirt in the shower. They had a washer/dryer set in the back apartment of the club, so she'd ask Luce if she could use it.

She bagged up her wet clothes and one small towel and headed back to the garage. She'd have to settle for an apple and candy bar she'd bought at the petrol station for breakfast. She had to work at three o'clock, so she had the entire morning to drive the city, looking for a needle in a haystack. She'd check their old neighborhood, drive by her old flat, and then go to the last place her father had lived.

* * *

Jack hopped off the train at Cambridge to find Katherine waiting for him. She'd kept quiet until they got to the office.

A building with no markers indicating that it was a satellite MI5 station. When they got to her office, she turned her computer screen around to reveal some security footage from their holding facility. "Mick Tierney. a.k.a. Michael Rufus Tierney. Mother was Irish, father was from Blackpool. He's lived in London for twenty-eight years. A long standing member of the Sons of the Fallen. He's been in custody for six days."

"How the hell did you pull that off? He didn't get counsel or call anyone?"

"He hasn't been given access to those things. He has ties to the IRA, so given the terrorist link, we are holding him due to national security concerns."

Jack laughed bitterly. "Well, that is a stretch. Don't let the BBC get hold of that story."

"The BBC couldn't give two shits about a white, male, two-bit biker. We made it work, however, which is lucky for you."

"Anything useful from him? Did he give up Clyde?"

"No. He's as tight lipped as a nun. We need a way in. He seems to have nothing to lose. Nothing we can hold over his head. He doesn't appear to be afraid of prison. I think he knows we don't have a strong case against him. Our intel was from an incarcerated associate in Belfast. Our goal is Bobby Clyde. You know this." Jack thought about Luce, so calculating and a bit paranoid. But he had a competent, commanding presence and a sharp wit which bred loyalty in his men.

"He has no family?" Jack asked.

"His wife is dead. Twenty years ago, she was found dead with a bullet in her head on the banks of the Thames. He never remarried. Parents are dead. He has a sister who lives in Surrey. She's clean. Not even a parking ticket."

"He was married, though. He looks young for having had a wife twenty years ago."

She slid a file to him across the desk. "He's forty-seven, so old enough. His wife was Annalise Tierney, maiden name O'Maolin. She grew up in Belfast."

He sharpened up. "Irish? That makes sense. Rose had a cousin that was friends with him. It's how she found the club. He must have the Irish connections from his dead wife."

"Rose, you say? Well, that's interesting. Keep reading."

His neck prickled as he read it again out loud. "Two children. Unknown whereabouts. Rose Tierney born in 1992 and Kieran Tierney born in 1999. They were six years apart. Twenty years ago she'd have been six, he'd have been a small baby. Jesus. He's not a friend of the family, he's her father. He sent them away when his wife died."

"You mean when she was murdered," Katherine said grimly.

"I need to talk to him."

"Not happening. If we can't hold him, you're still in the field. Let me count the ways that isn't happening, Jackson. Give me everything you have and I will work it from a new angle. Meanwhile, you need to cozy up to the daughter. I know you're a bit rusty, but she may know something. She's been off the radar for how long, and now she shows up?"

"Couldn't have anything to do with her father going incommunicado?" he said wryly.

"Perhaps." She shrugged, "Regardless, use her. The mother's murder is a cold case. They suspect a rival gang, but I'm going to try to find the old case file from the London police. Rose was six years old. She's bound to remember the incident. It's time to turn on the charm and maybe she'll open up. Meanwhile, I'll call the Belfast office and have them look into the O'Maolin family. That's likely where he dropped the children." He just stood there, hands on his hips, looking at nothing. "What's bothering you?"

"I don't know, really. It's this woman. She doesn't fit the mold for one of those women that frequent biker bars. She lied to Luce, which takes some pretty big bollocks. Why not just ask him where her father was?"

"I don't know. If she knows what happened to her mother, I can see why she'd be hesitant to tip her hand. What do you mean she doesn't fit the mold?"

He exhaled. "You'd maybe have to be a man to understand it. She's fresh and young. She's not polluted. She shouldn't be mixed up in this. These men are animals. It's like Sodom and Gomorrah in that bloody clubhouse. I don't want any collateral damage on this case."

Katherine clapped him on the shoulder. "She's not your problem. If you have to use her to get to Tierney or Clyde, then do it."

* * *

ROSE WAS uncomfortable as she watched the man who'd come in an hour earlier. He had Candice on his lap, but she kept catching him staring at her. He had dead eyes, and she had to resist the urge to shudder when he lifted a hand for another refill. He was Luce's second in command, and people called him Hammer. He was wiry and rough looking, with a big nose and a harsh face, and hair that needed to be cut five years ago. He was older than Luce, who she'd heard through the grapevine was turning fifty. They were planning a real piss-up in his honor. Probably flowing tequila and drugs, plenty of women. She was working, of course. Always the same departure time. The money was good, though. He rounded up her hours and paid her cash, which she needed. She had electricity in the garage. One outlet where she could plug in a hot plate. She needed to eat more. After a few days of living rough, she could already tell she was losing weight. Then again, maybe that was from walking a block to the bloody loo twice a night. She was exhausted and her body felt ancient. She wanted her bed, back home. If she stayed much longer, she was just going to have to risk it and come clean with Luce. She needed to find her da.

She'd called home late this morning. Her granny had been taking her mid-morning nap, and Kieran had answered. *I know you lied to Granny. Where are you? Why can't you tell me? Maybe I can help.* But he couldn't help. He'd never be able to live like this. He needed regular medical care and this house of ill repute was no place for him either. She looked up as she heard the door open. A few cheers for the well-favored patron.

"Jackknife! Did you come back for more, lad?"

He did look a little hungover. He looked stubbly and grungy and pretty much delicious. Dammit. He was not her type. At all. She liked good guys. Had never had a bad boy hang-up. Well, not since her school days. That had been a hard lesson to learn, but on the rare occasion she had a date, she liked her men clean cut and respectable. Boy scouts and superheroes. Not some feckin' biker who'd probably taken one of the whores to the back room last night. She cocked her head as he took a stool right in front of her. He was handsome. She could almost see the inner Boy Scout in his face. He looked to be a little older than her. Maybe thirty or so. "Hair of the dog?"

He smiled, and it was warm and just for her. She cursed in her head. "Yes. Thank you, Rose." And why the hell did he have to keep using her name like that? Like he knew her or wanted to know her. This guy was off the rails hot. She knew what she looked like. Not any great beauty, but she was in good shape and held her own in the cute department. But these boys liked them with lots of T & A and highlights and hotpants. She tugged on her peasant blouse, regretting it. Probably too Anne of Green Gables for this crowd. Shit. What on earth was she doing? And where the bloody hell was her father? She had a life to get back to. She was sleeping in a filthy garage. Gran would have a seizure if she saw her right now. She shook herself, realizing he'd answered her, and that she was staring at him like an idiot. She poured the pint of bitter and saw Hammer with his tongue down Candice's throat. She looked away and heard, "This isn't the place for you, Rose. You need to think about getting another job." His voice was low and she met his eyes.

"I'm fine. And it isn't permanent."

"That's probably what Candice thought." She bristled and he raised a brow, challenging her to argue the point.

Jack was an idiot. He was supposed to be cozying up to this girl, not scaring her off. He hated this feeling. It was like watching a puppy get ready to run out into the road during rush hour traffic. And he really didn't like how Hammer was looking at her. He didn't like Hammer period. Luce had given the hands-off rule to the crew. It was obvious. She was beautiful and had the air of innocence that drove wicked men like flies to honey. But they barely looked at her, and he knew they'd been threatened by their commander. Hammer was another story. He was Luce's second, and he did as he pleased. Jack wasn't confident that Luce would step in if Hammer really decided to put the moves on her. "Rose, it's going to storm tonight. Your tires need replacing. How are you getting home?"

She didn't look up. "I have it handled. Don't worry yerself over me, Jackknife. Just drink your beer."

"That's not an answer. Do you have a way home that doesn't involve hydro-planing into a bloody light pole?"

They were interrupted by Hammer yelling for a couple of shots of Tequila, and she ghosted away to get it.

* * *

JACK LEFT the pub a couple of hours before her shift ended, switching to a shitty, eight-year-old Peugeot SW that he borrowed from his mother's cook. When he'd offered up his keys to the Jaguar, Judith had almost had a stroke, but he'd assured her that she was doing him a favor by trading for a few days. It wouldn't do to have him seen driving the Jag. He rushed back from Chelsea and then he waited. He knew she wouldn't take a ride from him outright. He could hardly blame her, given the clientele in the clubhouse. He knew why Luce made her leave before eleven. Some of the men came in to talk business and get their marching orders. Some dealers, some security. They'd had trouble with a rival gang in the past. When there wasn't business at hand, the serious partying started. Copious amounts of alcohol, some coke or weed, and Candice and some of the other girls doing what they did best in the back rooms, or on some occasions, right in plain view. It was petty stuff, mainly, and not enough to take the club down, or its owner. They were looking for a major bust. Something to keep Bobby Clyde, a.k.a. Luce, in prison for the rest of his adult life. Murder or a major drug or gun trafficking charge. They needed to find his stash. Or catch him in the midst of a large transaction with his supplier. Not an easy thing. Jack was on the fringes, as his brother had been. They would sell to him, but they wouldn't let him in their inner circle. Luce was paranoid, too. No cell phones in the club. He laughed at the thought of some millennial-filled pub banning smartphones in London, but Luce didn't fuck around. Likely he was worried about someone taking pictures or video.

Rose likely knew nothing, but her father was right in the middle of it. By rights, he should be the second in command. According to Katherine, he didn't use drugs. He was smart. Way smarter than Hammer. Hammer was a thug. Luce was a mixture of the two. As shrewd as he was brutal.

As much as he hated it, Katherine was right. He was going to have to use Rose. He'd start by figuring out where she was staying because she was supposed to be living in Ballyclare with her granny. The encrypted email that Katherine had sent to his phone had confirmed it. Rose and Kieran Tierney had been given over to the care of their maternal grandmother. They'd found the regular payments to her, child support, from Mick's account. They were continuing to dig. The brother would be about nineteen, which put Rose at twenty-six. Much older than he'd first thought. Not that much younger than himself. Not that it mattered what their age difference was...really.

THE RAIN WAS COMING down in solid sheets, and the roads were starting to hold a layer of water as the storm sewers got overwhelmed. This close to the river, she hoped like hell the Thames didn't jump the bank. Luckily, most of the streets were fairly free of traffic. Just a few cars coming and going. The only issue was visibility. She had to go slow. Her helmet was keeping her head dry, but the shield kept blurring over. She really needed to get a car someday. She loved her Triumph, but this was downright dangerous. A car passed her and shot water up from the tires and splashed all over her. She was soaked to the bone. Her leather jacket only did so much without a hood. The water leaked in through the collar, trickling down her back and between her breasts until she was wet all over. As she went through a green light, she saw her life flash before her as a BMW started sliding into the intersection and straight for her. She swerved, which helped her avoid the car, but made her lose her traction on the road. Next thing she knew, she was laying it down. It wasn't a fast crash, but just enough to feel her jeans tear and her entire side hit the pavement.

Jack watched in horror as Rose laid her bike down. He slammed the brakes on, going for his door when she was on her feet. Jesus Christ. She was a lunatic! He could barely see in this family car with all of its safety features and big windows. He heard her screaming at the driver who just took off without a backward glance. Then she was on her bike again. He swore with feeling. His mother would be appalled at the language he'd been picking up with this new assignment. Her bike engine roared to life, and it hadn't escaped him that she was moving stiffly. He couldn't see much, other than she'd obviously felt that hit to the ground, but wasn't mortally wounded. She continued, and he followed, feeling like the worst sort of tosser for not jumping out of his car and demanding the little hellcat let him drive her to the hospital for x-rays. He needed to see where she was staying, however. He had no way of getting to her other than under the watchful eye of Luce and the other club members.

She didn't go much farther. It was a dodgy part of town. Old houses, trash turned over in the alleys. Jack watched as she stopped at a rather shabby looking two story. She dismounted her bike, and he could tell she was feeling that crash. He squeezed the steering wheel as he watched her from down the alley. She opened the old garage door, pulled her bike inside, and closed it. Then he saw the light come on. A lantern of sorts, as well as a hanging lamp, like the kind mechanics use that was on retractable cord and hung from above. What the hell? She must be checking out her bike. She seemed to be taking a long time. A really long time and he started to worry that maybe she was really hurt. He got out of the car, pulling his collar up around his neck. Then he crept over to get a better look.

Rose was so tired. So bloody tired and now sore. She looked at her bike. It was scuffed on the right side, but no major damage. She'd only been going about fifteen kph when she'd laid it down. Her jeans, on the other hand, were done for. The hip had a large tear in it, and she was reminded why experienced bikers wore leather chaps. The abrasion on her hip stung where the pants had peeled away, and her shoulder was screaming. She wasn't badly injured. Not to the point of needing a hospital. She took out the small medical kit she kept in her saddlebag and moved away from the window to strip her wet clothes off. She put on some soft yoga pants because she was chilled to the bone. Then she slid on a warm hooded jumper. She really needed to get some more clothes. She'd traveled light, in hopeful expectation of finding her father within a few days. She moved back into the light and began dressing her wounds.

When Jack saw her reveal the wound on her hip, he cursed to himself. She seemed to be proficient with the medical kit, however. He also noticed she was shaking. Whether from adrenalin or her core temperature dropping, he didn't know. Why on earth was she doing this out in the garage? Why didn't she go inside the house? That's when he saw it. A bedroll and backpack. She used a bowl and a bottle of water to wash up and brush her teeth. He started to shake then. What in the hell would cause this young, beautiful girl to hide out in a garage in London instead of being at home with her family in Ireland? He watched her take the lantern over, and her whole body was shaking as she crawled into the sleeping bag.

Fuck this. Before he thought better of it, he was banging

on the side door to the garage. The light went out and she didn't come. More knocking. "Rose, I know you're in there. It's Jack. I mean Jackknife." He knocked again. "Rose, I'm not leaving. I am not some psychopath. I want to make sure you're okay. Stop being so goddamn stubborn! I can wait out here all night and wake the neighborhood, or you can open the door." The light came on and she transformed from the wounded pup to the she-lion. Her face was murderous. She whipped open the door and grabbed him by the lapels. She winced then, forgetting her shoulder. "Christ, woman! Have you lost your senses? You're hurt. I followed you home." She took a step back. He put his hands up to put her at ease and added, "Just to make sure you got home okay. I knew you wouldn't accept a ride and it was pouring out, so I drove back to the club."

She pointed in his face. "Good intentions or not, it isn't your feckin' business where I go or how I get there. I can't believe you followed me!"

She put her finger back down when she noticed her tremors. His face softened as he looked around. "And get that look off your face. This is temporary. I'm not some gutter rat you need to rescue."

He exhaled. "Rose, you came down hard. You're injured." He touched her wrist before she could retract it. "Christ, woman. You're chilled to the bone. You cannot sleep on the floor of this garage." He took in the three buckets filling from the leaking roof. His voice grew calm. "Be reasonable. I'm sorry I invaded your privacy, but you don't seem to have anyone looking after you."

"I don't need anyone. I'm a grown woman!"

"Who's sleeping rough in a derelict garage?"

She stopped short, suddenly realizing something. "Your accent...it's different."

He stiffened. "You must have hit your head as well."

"I know what I heard. Who the hell are you?"

His phone went off and she put her hands on her hips. "Your mobile is ringing."

He knew who it was. Katherine. She was supposed to call tonight with a brief on Rose's relations in Ballyclare. He gestured to her bag. "Get your belongings. I'll take you to a hotel." She started to argue. It occurred to him that she couldn't afford it, and she wasn't going to let him pay. "Actually, I have a friend who's out of the country. His place is nicer than a hotel. It's in Convent Garden, in a better neighborhood. I was housesitting, but I'll let you use it until we figure something out."

"You don't even know me! You can't just give me the keys to some random bloke's flat!"

"Get your belongings sorted or I swear to God I will stuff you in the boot. You won't get out until we are at the house." He opened the door and said. "Five minutes. Bring everything. We'll get your motorbike later."

Rose watched the arrogant bastard walk out the door and into the rain. She looked out the window to see him run to a modest looking car. That was singly the strangest conversation of her life. He'd followed her. Although that should creep her out, she had to admit it was kind of sweet. It had been stupid of her to try riding home on such a night. Foolish and dangerous. But that wasn't the weirdest part. What was up with his manner of speech? Most of the time, he had the rougher multi-cultural London English of the millennial generation. Not full blown cockney, with its missing *h*s and *t*s. More a middle ground, urban sort of slang for this new generation of working class Londoner. But as he grew more frustrated with her, his words had not become rougher. Quite the opposite. He'd slipped into the quintessential BBC London accent, with clear and articulate words. He'd gone from Hagrid to Hermoine and hadn't even realized it. His words had changed as well. Motorbike instead of bike, belongings instead of stuff. Like he'd had a mouth transplant.

Now he was taking her to Convent Garden. She'd never been to London until last week, but she'd driven the city a bit, and she'd done her research on the layout of the city before she'd left Ireland. It was a very nice part of London. Too rich for his blood, or so he'd have her believe. It didn't add up. One thing was for certain. He was playing a role for the crowd at Luce's. The question was, why?

Jack was close to smashing his head into the steering wheel, he was so pissed off. He rang Katherine, trying to blot out the horrendous blunder he'd just made in front of Rose Tierney. He knew better. The problem was, although he could blend in with the other side of the tracks, he was used to blending with the polar opposite. His polished, articulate, private school diction fit right in when he was hobnobbing with the elites of the high finance world. His mother wouldn't even be able to fault him there. And when a person got stressed or emotional, their native tongue and accent grew more pronounced. He'd slipped out of his East London accent in the heat of their argument, and she'd noticed.

"Katherine, what do you have?"

"Good evening to you as well, love. Where are you? Can you talk?"

"Yes, it took me a minute, but I'm alone."

Katherine said, "I've gathered some more information about the daughter and son." She slowed at the end of the sentence.

"And? Go on. "

"They are living with their maternal grandmother in Ballyclare, just as you overheard. The investigator didn't look there because Annalise O'Maolin grew up in Belfast. He wasn't overly thorough, I'm afraid."

"Okay, so why do you sound like you are preparing to deliver bad news?" he asked.

"It's nothing to do with the case. It has more to do with why Rose might be looking for her father. Apparently, they've been estranged since she left England."

"Would you please not make me drag this out of you? I've had an off night."

"It's her brother, Jack. He's got stage three leukemia. Apparently…" she paused, sighing. "Apparently it's not looking good. He's a rare blood type and he needs a bone marrow transplant. I'm assuming she's out of options and wants the father to get tested, or maybe look for more blood relatives on this side of the sea."

Jack felt like he got kicked in the bollocks. "Fucking hell."

"Right. I hesitated even telling you, but I thought it might come up if you got close to her. Nigel thinks perhaps you can use it."

"You're joking, right? Are you trying to get me into Hell?"

"It would certainly be useful on our end. He's got an incentive to get out of custody."

"They can't just keep him. Surely they know this. He's a British citizen. If he doesn't give up something soon, you've got to let him go."

"Listen, I know you thought you had the stomach for this. I know this is personal, but if you want out…"

"No. I need to go. Thanks for the information."

"Jack, wait." She paused, treading carefully. "I realize that I am the one who told you to cozy up to this woman, but be careful. You can't tip your hand just yet. I feel terrible for the family. They've got nothing to do with this lot in London. It's obvious. But we don't know where her loyalties will fall if it comes down to it."

CHAPTER 3

*J*ack should have expected the contrary wench to fight him, but he was still a little surprised when he came in and she hadn't gathered her things. He rubbed his palm over his face. "Is there a problem?"

"Yes, you're keeping me awake. You need to leave."

"Rose..."

"Stop saying that!" Rose shook herself.

"Stop saying your name? That doesn't make any sense, Rose." He paused right before and practically crooned her name, just to irritate her. He was smiling, because now that she was illuminated by that garage light, he noticed how completely stunning she was when she was angry. Like a pretty little red hen, wet and bristly. He shouldn't be goading her, but being thoughtful and protective hadn't worked. His limited experience with Irish women taught him that they liked to fight it out and they were extremely prideful. So he'd let her fight him a little, get it out of her system.

She approached him, attempting to grow taller. "Move along. I'm sure I'll see you tomorrow since you seem to enjoy slumming it with the rest of us."

He cocked his head. "What is that supposed to mean?"

"It means that you don't belong there or here. Shouldn't you be married with a couple of tow-headed babes at home? Nice station wagon, by the way."

He cracked off a laugh, which she hadn't been expecting. "Christ, talk about living up to stereotypes. Do you have to argue about everything? You're fucking shaking, you're so bloody cold. I'd like to think you're trembling because you're so close to all this feral masculinity." He motioned up and down his body. "But your body temperature is in the basement, you're living in a garage with no heat, living off nuts and bars," he said, lifting up a wrapper from her workstation, "and that bucket just filled to the overflow point and is running all over your cot," he said as he pointed.

She turned around and swore loudly. "No, no, no!" She snatched her sleeping bag off the ground and it dripped. She threw it against the wall of the garage. He watched her struggle to rein in the meltdown that was threatening. Fists clenched, jaw tight, fighting tears.

He said nothing. He knew what it was like to feel like the universe had singled you out for an ass beating. He thought of her brother, and why she was here looking for her father. He thought about watching her go down on that death machine she called a motorbike.

He calmly took her backpack and the wet sleeping bag. "Grab your wet clothes. There's a dryer at the house." He walked out the door, popped open the umbrella that his mother's cook, Judith, kept in her station wagon, and he waited. He hated watching the defeat creep over her features. He actually liked that she was a fighter. He admired her. She picked up her wet clothes and followed, straightening her shoulders and lifting her chin as she walked under the protection of his umbrella.

* * *

"This isn't your car." She was smart, he'd give her that.

"And how did you come to that conclusion?" he asked calmly.

"It smells like smoke, and you don't. It also has one of these." She pinged the air freshener with her finger. "No one under the age of sixty uses these anymore." He smiled. "Why are you smiling? You're a liar. Some sort of London chancer that I shouldn't be goin' anywhere with."

"You're going with me because you've finally come to your senses. You are correct. My car's in the shop, and no one in their right mind would ride a motorbike in this rain." He said, just to take a jab at her. "I borrowed it from a friend of the family until my car is fixed.

"Really? And what do you drive? Specifically."

Shit. He paused just long enough to make her snort. "You can drop me off at a local hostel. I've got enough cash for the night and Convent Garden is too far for me to get to work every day."

"And what about tomorrow? What will you do for housing tomorrow?"

"Luce pays me nightly. I'll be perfectly fine. I was trying to avoid paying for lodgings until I get settled, but it appears the rain has defeated me and my little hovel." She saw the international hostel sign illuminated in the distance. "Just there, two blocks ahead. That'll do."

He said flippantly, "No vacancy. Sorry. But I have a brilliant alternative." She turned in her seat, eyes narrowed at him as he made a left turn. "How about you staying in a completely available, spotlessly clean, free alternative that some nice gentleman has offered to give you? Because he's a nice bloke, and he wants you to be safe?"

"Jesus, Joseph, and Mary! Why do you care?" Then she

stopped short. "If you're thinkin' I'll shed my knickers for nice accommodations, then you can stop this car now. If you want that, Candice would probably give you a discount!"

He gave her a chiding look. "Candice is a pathetic but very nice girl. You should pity her, not mock her. She's made some bad choices. Addicts do that."

She blew out a breath, rubbed her temples. "You're right. That wasn't nice. She's a lost soul, isn't she?" Then her eyes sharpened. "That aside, I'm no whore."

"I know that, Rose. Have I ever once treated you like one? You don't belong in that place. I wish you'd just let me help you. I don't want anything from you." He sighed, frustrated with himself and her. "Listen, I have a sister. I hate to think about her in your situation. You are obviously short of funds and you've got some reason for putting yourself through this, although I can't fathom what it is. I heard your interview. Your home in Ireland sounded nice. Safe. What the hell are you doing?" She clenched her jaw, looking away. "Rose, if you tell me what your end game is, maybe I can help you get there. Why did you come to London?"

She was quiet, and he paid the toll and kept on the route to his previous residence in Convent Garden. It was beautiful. In a gorgeous part of the city with lots of restaurants and art galleries. It was a better place for someone like her. He'd considered selling it, but he was attached to the place and his sister loved it. They went along in silence for a time, until he turned onto the tree-lined road toward his building. It had originally been built in 1826 but had seen many lives since then. He'd purchased three flats, straight up from one another, and done the construction to turn them into a three-story townhouse. The trend had caught on with the wealthier sect, and the entire building had been converted into similar setups. Where there had been fifteen separate apartments, there were now five large units. *Ever the trendset-*

ter, he thought with amusement as he parked in the covered garage.

As they approached with Rose's modest belongings in his hands, he warmed as he watched her face transform. "It's a gorgeous building. Which one is yours?" she said, looking up to the windows. He took her in a side entrance, a beautiful cornflower blue door that he'd purchased at auction to go with the original period of the building. He watched her stop and smell the deep red flowers that were in beds to the right and left of the steps. "Ye need to prune these a bit. Roses need tending. You don't want your friend coming home to find you've let his wee roses grow ragged."

His heart squeezed. His mother always made derogatory comments about the Irish. Actually, about anyone who wasn't rich and well-bred and from London. But he thought Rose's voice was lovely, and she had a natural beauty that stirred him. She didn't have the polished edge of the female Londoners in the corporate world. Power suits, cut to accentuate a waist that was honed in a private gym with a personal trainer. Sharp edges. Rose's curves were soft. He noticed she was favoring her one leg and blocked out the thought of her laying her bike down at that intersection.

He had to get a grip on his libido. She was crucial to this case. Crucial to bringing down the Sons of the Fallen. He couldn't let his mind wander into lustful thoughts about Rose. Katherine would have a fucking stroke if she knew he'd brought her to one of his properties. He was supposed to be working undercover. He'd just panicked, which wasn't like him. The crash, the fact that she was sleeping in a filthy garage in a dodgy neighborhood, and the news he'd heard about her brother, it had all clouded his judgment. He went in ahead of her and told her to have a seat on the couch. He ran up on the second floor, checking one of his two guest rooms. Then he went to the third floor that led to the master suite. Yes, this was it. This was perfect. She deserved this luxury. A pillow top mattress and a view of the city. He put her bag down, then returned to the bottom level. She was looking around the place and said, "Your mate's home is gorgeous altogether. I wish I had friends like this. Is this the bedroom?" She opened the door into an office.

"The bottom floor was blown out to accommodate the open kitchen. The bedroom was turned into a den and library." She smiled at that. "I always wanted a library. Gran's always complaining about my piles of books everywhere." He watched her and loved that she was so appreciative of his home. Well, at least one of them. His intention was to gift this to his sister when she graduated from college. "Come, I'll show you the other floors."

Rose was in love. This whole place was just so beautiful. Old world opulence, yet no trace of gaudiness. Leather books, beautiful art. "Do you play?" she said, as she ran her hand over the keys of the piano. An antique upright, nestled between two windows. The fireplace was huge on the other wall, with a gorgeous oak mantelpiece.

"No, I don't. The friend who owns it, his father played. He kept his piano because his mother was going to replace it with a grand."

"Aye, that must be one of those rich person problems that I've no reference for. I've an old spinet at my granny's house. It was my mother's."

"You speak of your mum in the past tense. Is she…" He trailed off, knowing damn well her mother was dead but needing to gain her trust. He felt like a rotter. It had never bothered him before, lying to his marks, but for some reason, it bothered him now.

"Yes, she's been gone for twenty years."

"And what of your father?"

"He's not in the picture. It's just me, my brother, and my gran."

"You have a sibling as well? Older or younger?" *You are such a lying piece of shit. She's going to hate you by the end of this.* He quelled that voice in his head as she answered.

"Younger. He was a baby when she died."

"Well, at least you remember her. You can fill in the blanks to a point. And your granny," he said, wanting to offer her something.

"Aye, well I can't actually. I don't remember her. It's strange. It's just a blank. I remember feelings. I remember smells and the touch of her hair on my face, but it's like the first six years barely happened. Gran says it was likely the loss that cut the memories away. That I couldn't process it. She's not very helpful, I'm afraid. I don't even know how she died."

"They never told you?" he asked, a sinking feeling that she wasn't going to be of aid in the murder cold case.

"No. Gran said she drowned in the river, but I don't believe her. Ye get to know someone after twenty years of sharing a space. She's a terrible liar. She doesn't have the soul for it."

An odd way to put it, he thought. "And what about you? Do you have the soul for it?"

She stiffened. "I should ask you the same. What are your intentions here, Jack?"

He prudently backed off. "A roof over your head and checking your injuries. As much as you're comfortable."

"I've checked them. I'll live."

"Do you think you're qualified to make that call?"

Rose smiled and answered, "Yes. I actually think I'm very qualified." She said no more, which had him wondering what she'd done in Ireland, before taking a job in that God forsaken clubhouse.

He closed in just a few inches. "Humor me, Rose. I saw you go down. You're favoring a leg and you wince when you use the shoulder. And by the look of your trousers, you probably need to clean your abrasions and bandage them."

She sighed. She knew he was right. "I'll do that, thank you. As for the shoulder, it's going to hurt like hell, but I'm not experiencing any swelling. The leather and the helmet did their job. I may need some chaps if I'm going to keep riding in the rain, however. They're a bit dear, so I've put it off."

"Yes, well maybe one of the ladies at the club has a used pair." He smiled. "Actually, given the after-hours events, I'm sure more than one woman has left her clothing behind." Fuck that for a laugh. He was going to get her a pair of chaps. And new tires. He told himself that he couldn't have his potential star witness in a coma from another accident, but the truth was more revealing. He wanted her safe.

He took her elbow in his hand and cupped her shoulder. "All right, lift it straight up. How far can you go?" She lifted it and winced when she got the elbow even with her shoulder. "Yes, I'm sorry. That must hurt. Okay, roll it." She did, and he felt her tighten, saw her jaw clench."

"You should have an x-ray."

"If it swells or seems to worsen, I will. A bit of ice should help."

He went to the kitchen, opened the freezer, and took out an ice pack. "Ye have an ice pack ready?"

He smiled. "My sister is a dancer. A very talented, driven, stubborn dancer. The ballet is a brutal way to make a living. I've got ice packs everywhere."

"You're a good brother," she said.

And you're a good sister, he thought. The brother had to be the reason she was putting herself through this. "I like to think so. I've been neglecting her. Our schedules don't match up, I'm afraid. She's on a pretty vigorous rehearsal schedule. She's trying out for the Royal Ballet." Rose lifted her brows. "Yeah, as I said, she is extremely talented and driven."

"And stubborn," Rose filled in the rest.

"Yes, quite. It's the way of it with strong women." He smiled as she lifted her chin. His hands were still on her shoulder, and all he'd have to do is move them and run his hands in that silky hair. Take her beautiful mouth like he wanted to. But that was not going to happen. He'd already crossed several lines with her. He had her in one of his homes. He was talking about his sister. Everything he'd been taught not to do. He put space between them, letting go of her arm as gently as he could. "Help yourself to anything. I'm afraid all I have is tins of food and a few items in the freezer. No produce to speak of. I come and go and haven't been cooking." Actually, he'd moved out two months ago, but he kept a little food in case he slept here. "I'll call the cleaning staff and tell them to stay away. If you need them, however, just call me."

He took a notepad out of the drawer. Writing down his alternate cell that he used on the job, he looked at her. "I'll be here at one if that's okay. You'll need a ride to work."

"I need my bike. You said…"

"And I'll get it."

"Just take me to it. I'll ride it to work."

He shook his head. "You're out of your mind. This rain is supposed to continue through tomorrow. You need new tires and you're injured. Give it a couple of days, Rose."

"Don't you have to be somewhere? I don't even know what you do for a living! This is ludicrous. I can take care of myself. I'm not your responsibility."

Yes, you are. He shook that thought away. "Here are the keys. Lock the doors. Your bag is on the third floor. Go rest, Rose." Then he thought about it. "There's tea, but there's also an espresso machine. The coffee is in the freezer. No milk, I'm afraid. You'll have to drink it Italian style." He walked over to a copper machine that looked like it was from a star trek movie. "It's not complicated. Well, actually it is, but…"

"I've had many jobs in my days as a student, Jack. Barista being one of them. I'll sort it out." She caught herself too late.

"Student? What did you study?"

Shit, she thought to herself. She was supposed to be a barmaid. "This and that. As I said, I'll figure it out." If she could work a defibrillator, she could make espresso.

He stared, as if taking her measure. Then he let it go. "There are several toiletries in the master bath. And some soaking oils that might help that hip. Best lay off the salts until it scabs over. It's a nice tub. Relax and sleep in. You've had a rough week, I'd wager. That garage floor didn't look very welcoming."

Rose looked away, suddenly ashamed of how he'd found her living like a street urchin. "I'm not homeless. I didn't think I'd be there more than a day or two, and my family needs my spare income. I have a home in Ireland. A modest one, but it's clean and well kept. I'm not some charity case."

He came in close then and turned her chin to meet his eyes. Gentle enough that she could move away if she wished. "I didn't think that you were. I just want to help. This place is empty, and I won't have to keep moving from my place to this one if you're here. It works for both of us."

She nodded and he moved away. He said, "I'll leave you to it, then. The laundry is off the second-floor bath, between the two bedrooms. It doesn't appear you have many clothes with you. If you need something, there are some old t-shirts in the dresser of the master. I keep some clothes here for workouts. There's an elliptical and some weights off the kitchen."

"Your friend seems to have it all."

"No one has it all. Everyone has pieces that are missing, Rose. Stuff money doesn't buy."

"Oh yes? Like what?"

"Honor. Duty. A sense of purpose." That's what he'd gotten from MI5. What his father had gotten from the military.

Rose understood. It's what she gained from nursing. "I suppose I can't argue with that. Surprising to hear you say it, considering where you spend your days."

"Ditto."

She smirked. He had her there. He turned to leave. "One o'clock. I'll bring you some lunch."

ROSE SIGHED as she cleared the third-floor landing. Holy God. The entire floor had been blown out into a sitting room and master bedroom. A bed the size of a rugby field that was in front of a sprawling row of windows. She could look over this section of the city. How the other half lived. He had one hell of a housesitting gig.

She went to her bag and picked it up with her good shoulder. Then she headed for what could only be the bath. She dropped it as she took a gander at the tub. She'd been expecting a jetted number, to go with the renovations. Instead, it was copper. An obvious custom made reproduction because it was huge. Lined with porcelain, probably pounded around cast iron. It looked like one of those old Victorian baths that some maid would fill and empty, with a high back where the bather would lean. At the foot, a brass fixture jutted up from the floor, the only clue that it was indeed modern plumbing. Heated floors that he must have turned on when he'd run upstairs. Jesus. This place was like nothing she'd ever even conceived of in her imagination. She couldn't believe people lived like this. The floor was marble and blue lapis mosaic. Gorgeous. She went to the cupboard and found tea tree oil, better as an antiseptic, and began filling the tub.

She stripped and sank into the warm water, wincing both at the pressure on her shoulder, and her hip hitting the water. She was already turning black and blue. Dammit. It was foolish of her not to call for a lift. She had some cash now. She thought about how the evening had progressed from there. He'd followed her to make sure she was safe. He hadn't expected anything from her, even though he'd put her up for the night. He hadn't even hit on her. She wasn't sure how she felt about that. She was glad he wasn't a rotter that would try to take advantage, but he was also stupidly gorgeous. He was tall and well built. He had hair that was thick and chestnut. His eyes were dark blue, like a stormy sea. Almost gray. His hands on her were gentle, and that made it all the more devastating. She was really in trouble if he decided to put the moves on her because she wasn't sure she'd stop him. She really didn't need that sort of complication right now. Her fantasy life had always been better than the real thing, anyway. The real thing had been a bitter disappointment.

She dressed for sleep and crawled into the clean bed. The mattress was perfect. Like a hug. Cotton sheets, down pillows and comforter. As she rolled into the pillow, she caught a scent. Pillows held scent, even if you laundered the linen. It was masculine. She'd smelled him when he'd been close. When he was checking her shoulder. This was his pillow, not the owner of the house.

Her arousal was instant. She inhaled deeply and felt a moan threaten. He smelled so good. Like pure male. She felt her legs scissor and she rolled on her stomach. She hadn't felt remotely sexual in a long time. She was always so tired and stressed, but right now, she felt it. Even with her injuries. Then she did something she hadn't done in a long time. She pictured his blue eyes and moaned as she felt herself fly apart like she was soaring over the city below.

* * *

HE'D BEEN UP and down all night. He was exhausted as he drank his morning tea and looked over the river. His mind had vacillated between scenes of her crashing on that fucking motorbike and better images of her in that copper tub. Or better yet, in his big bed. That was the path to madness because that led to all sorts of thoughts about what he'd like to do to her in that bed. He was such a bastard. She'd been very clear that his help must not come with strings attached, and he had to keep himself in line. Not to mention the more important issue of it being completely out of line for him to be shagging the daughter of the man they had in custody.

He took a tepid shower, not willing to put himself through a cold one, and headed to Cambridge. Katherine had called him in again. They had information on the cold case murder of Rose's mother. They were going to interview Tierney, and she wanted him to listen in. He made a quick call to his brother's motorcycle mechanic. The one who'd helped him with the custom paint and maintenance, now that he'd inherited the beast. The shop owner was going to arrange to pick up Rose's Triumph and check it over. As well as put new tires on it. She'd be pissed, but that was just too bad. If she was going to use it as her only transportation, rain or shine, the tires were the least that needed to happen.

The trip to the field office was a pain, and he regretted not taking a train. The rain was still coming down, and he was driving Judith's damn station wagon again. He really missed his Jag.

* * *

MICK TIERNEY WAS an intense looking man. He was tall with long legs and heavily muscled arms that were covered in tattoos. He was darker than Rose, with black hair and tanned skin...but those eyes. Katherine let Jack watch the interview from the one-way glass, unwilling to let Mick see him. Right now, Tierney looked like his head was going to explode. "What the hell do you mean, my daughter is in London?"

Nigel was cool as a cucumber. "Just as I said. Apparently she's working at your clubhouse. Is there a chance she's looking for you?"

"She's got no business in that club. You need to let me out. I want a bloody lawyer!"

Nigel ignored him and continued, "Because I have a suspicion why she's here. I have to say, you keep rather nasty company, but I never pegged you as quite so cold-hearted. Your own son, and you ignored her calls."

Mick's face blanched. "What are you talking about?"

"Am I wrong? She did call you a couple of weeks ago. I have the phone records."

"You've had me locked up for over a fucking week! I never got to speak to her. What the hell is this about?"

Nigel showed the first genuine surprise. "My word, old boy. Is it possible you don't know?" He looked at Katherine, and she just shrugged. "Rose is looking for you because she needs to have you tested as a match for bone marrow. How can you not know that your son has stage three leukemia? Did you really just write them off twenty years ago? Christ, you are cold aren't you?"

For the first time in his career, Jack actually felt sorry for the sod they had in custody. He watched Mick Tierney split down the middle. His chocolate eyes sparked as he went completely apeshit. Jack turned and walked out of the room, needing to block out the man's screams.

After a few minutes, Nigel and Katherine joined him. He turned on Nigel. "You are a real bastard, you know that? Despite what he's done, that boy is innocent. You need to get a fucking team in here and test him if you are going to hold him."

Nigel just raised a brow. "My, my. Consorting with bikers is eroding your manners, Jackson. I fully intend to have him taken to a medical facility at midnight, after hours. We'll get the blood and tissue samples to the hospital in Belfast within a day. That aside, the man in there is the enemy. He might not be as bad as Bobby Clyde, but his hands have filth all over them. This was necessary. I need him vulnerable. I'm going to let him stew for an hour and then I'll share my second bit of news."

Jack straightened. "What news? About the family?"

"No, about the dead wife. Twenty years ago, I was a brand new agent, not even out of training. We had a gang war that the old-timers still talk about. I dug into the cold case of Annalise O'Maolin-Tierney. She was beaten, choked, and then shot in the head, followed by the disposal of her body in the river. The word was that a rival gang had taken her out. The Outlaws suffered the retaliation for that, losing two members. We don't have any evidence, but one could assume that Mick Tierney was their judge and jury. The Fallen lost one. A low ranking prospect. They never pinned the murders to anyone specific. No one bothered to look into Mrs. Tierney's murder past the initial month or so. They assumed the culprits were dead at the hands of their rivals."

"So what have you found out? What's changed?"

"Katherine went through the case file and found a statement from one of the Outlaws. Jimmy Brooks, whose club name was Skids. He swears up and down that the Outlaws had nothing to do with the murder of Annalise Tierney. He seems to think that her murder was at the hands of her own club. One of the Fallen. They filed it away, writing it off as bollocks. Then he shows up again, doing hard time in the federal prison. He was trying to get his sentence reduced. He tells the same story, and then says that he knew who killed the prospect. The one that was a retaliation hit. He was doing time for murder. They wouldn't deal, so he never gave up the name. All he said was that it wasn't one of his men."

"Are you telling me that he thinks that the prospect and Rose's mother were killed by one of Tierney's M.C. brothers?"

"I have no bloody idea. All I know is that it's enough to sow a seed of dissension between the club and Mick Tierney. That's the second blow that might make him talk."

* * *

JACK PULLED into the parking garage and sat for a minute, trying to get his mind into character. He'd dropped off the car in Battersea, switching to his bike. The rain had stopped just over an hour ago, and the sky was beginning to clear. He didn't want to show up to the club in the housewife special he'd been driving.

He also needed to erase from his thoughts how he'd spent his morning. Jesus, what a shit time. Rose seemed like a good woman. Far above all of this bloody business. He thought about how her mother died and it made his insides curl with tension. He wanted her out of that club. If the worst was true, someone from that motorcycle club had brutally murdered a young, defenseless woman and made it look like a rival gang.

50

They didn't suspect the husband, Rose's father. They'd tried that angle in the original investigation, but he had an ironclad alibi. He'd been in Surrey at his sister's home. Her husband was a local copper, and he'd accounted for Mick's whereabouts during the murder. He'd also included in the statement that although Mick kept rough company, he was a devoted father and husband. That he was a good lad who had fallen in with an unfortunate group of men. At forty-seven, Tierney had obviously been a pup when he'd married and started a family. And when he'd gotten mixed up with the Sons of the Fallen.

He walked up to the house and decided that he'd best ring the doorbell. Rose was wary of him, he knew. Suspicious of his intentions. And although he owned this home, she didn't know that. He wasn't just going to barge in on her without announcing himself.

What he really wanted to do was kick the door in like a barbarian and haul her up to that big bed. He was stressed, and he had an edge to him right now that could be honed with some vigorous bed play. He should call one of his casual lays. A woman who didn't want anything from him other than some great sex. He was too raw to be around Rose right now. But the thought of being with another woman made him sick. He'd slept like shit last night, imagining her sprawled across that bed. Imagining kissing her everywhere, tasting her as she writhed under his mouth. He swore under his breath as he heard her coming down the stairs to the front door. She opened the door and took a step back.

"Ye look in a right foul mood, Jack. What is it, then?"

He shook himself, "Nothing, sorry. Just a bit hungry." He held up the bag of take-away and she smiled.

"Is that curry I smell?" Her face lit up and his mood immediately shifted. He'd done something to make her smile. And he was a fucking sap, so it made him smile as well. "The best in London. Do you mind if I join you? I just grabbed it and came straight over."

Her face blushed so sweetly. "It's not even my home. Of course, you can come in." He stepped through the door and stopped short, taking in what she was wearing. She had one of his shirts on. His Cambridge rowing t-shirt.

She seemed to realize what he was thinking. "Oh, my clothes are in the wash. You said I could…" Her face reddened and she said, "I'll go take it off."

He touched her forearm gently as she turned. "No, don't. It suits you. About ten sizes too large, but it suits you just the same." He liked her in his shirt.

"Is it your friend's shirt, then? The one who owns the house? Everything was the same size and I just grabbed the softest thing."

"It's mine." She raised her brows. He was an idiot. He should be covering, but he just couldn't bring himself to tell her one more fucking lie. "Scholarships."

'What the hell is a Cambridge graduate doing hanging out at Luce's?"

Why is a college graduate with a nursing degree doing the same? He thought the words but didn't say them. He'd read the rest of the file they'd compiled on Mick Tierney's family. Rose had just graduated magna cum laude from nursing school. He could just see her, serious and competent, in little blue scrubs. Jesus, he wanted to fake a heart attack right now just for a shot at mouth to mouth. "What about you, Rose? You said you'd studied this and that? Any particular coursework?"

He watched her trying to weigh how much she should tell him. "Actually, I just graduated. I haven't even started working. I'm officially a registered nurse as of a few weeks ago."

It shouldn't please him as much as it did that she'd been honest. "A nurse? I'm not surprised. It's a noble profession.

Why the hell aren't you back in Ireland putting it to good use? Why are you here, Rose?"

She turned from him, taking out dishes to plate the take-out. "Why do you need to know?"

"I don't. But I'd like to know just the same. I'd like to help you. Maybe if you told me why then I could."

Rose couldn't take this man standing in front of her. He was big and gorgeous and apparently, he was also smart. Cambridge, for feck sake. She sighed. Too much time was passing. She was going to have to come clean with Luce. She thought she'd be here for a couple of days, and she'd been here almost a week. Then her grandmother had called this morning. Kieran was back in the hospital. He was fighting a mild case of pneumonia. But cancer patients weren't like everyone else. He wasn't as strong as a regular nineteen-year-old boy. Pneumonia could go bad fast. He'd been through a round of chemo and he was vulnerable. Suddenly her eyes welled up. *Oh, Kieran. You can't leave me. I will lay down and die right next to you.* She wasn't aware of him standing up until he was behind her, taking her shoulders gently in his hands to turn her.

"Rose, please."

She hadn't been held in so long. She'd forgotten what attraction and comfort felt like. Couldn't remember feeling both of those things together when it was from a man. She answered, "I need to find my da. He's in London. Or at least he was. I need to find him now."

"I thought you didn't have any dealings with him?"

"I haven't seen my da since I was six years old. After my mam died, he dropped us in Ireland and left. He said to never come looking for him, but I must find him. My brother is sick, Jack. I need to get my da to Ireland. He needs to see if he's a potential donor for bone marrow. My brother has a rare blood type. His leukemia is stage three and he needs a donor. I'm not a match. Siblings are supposed to be the best bet, but I don't fucking match! I'd drain my body dry for him if I could!"

Her voice was getting hysterical and he pulled her to him. This was gutting him. Both the lying and the fact that it made him think about his only remaining sibling. His sister was the beating heart in his chest. He understood all too well how precious a sibling was. "I'll help you, Rose. I promise. Why Luce's? Is your father a brother in the motorcycle club?"

She nodded. "Yes, but Luce is evading my questions. I'm starting to think that something happened. Luce is their president. He should know where his men are, but I think my da may be missing. I'm going to just come out with it and tell Luce."

God, he was such a bastard. He knew exactly where her father was. "I wouldn't do that. Not yet. I mean, those men are not to be trifled with. If your father has come to some sort of mischief, it might be their doing. Let me see what I can find out, Rose. Tomorrow night is Luce's big party. Everyone will be there. If your father is in town, maybe he'll show. Those men are savages, but they are like family. I think they'll all be there."

Rose thought about it. "Yes, you're right. He might come tomorrow. He missed every one of Kieran's birthdays, but he probably wouldn't miss Luce's." She hated that it bothered her, especially when she saw the cringe of pity wash over Jack. "If he doesn't, then I'll have to talk to Luce. He's a tough nugget, but he's not all bad. I think…"

Jack pulled her tight to him, on instinct. He was on pure male instinct right now, and he felt the danger she was in. "Do not be fooled by these men. Especially Luce. They seem like teddy bears when you're sliding them a pint down the bar, but they are not. They're dangerous. Rose, you need to listen to me."

Then he realized what he'd done. His hand was on the small of her back, the other between her shoulder blades. She was pressed tight against him and she was arching her neck, eyes wide, breaths coming short. Submissive. He almost roared. He wanted to protect her, yes. But he also wanted to lift her up on the counter and spread her thighs. Take her mouth, slow and deep. He backed off abruptly, needing to get his shit together. He'd been ready to kiss her. Ready to do more than that. What the fuck was wrong with him?

His voice was rough and strained. "Let's eat while this take-away is still warm. Then I'll take you to work."

"The rain stopped about an hour ago. Just take me to my bike."

"Your bike is in the shop." He watched her bristle and stood firm, returning her stubborn stare.

"You shouldn't have done that. God only knows what he's going to charge me!"

"He owes me a favor. Don't worry about the cost. He'll salvage some good tires, most likely."

"He owes you a favor, not me. And I'm not comfortable with you doing this for me. You've already done enough. It would be best if I left." She groaned inwardly. She didn't want to leave. That bed alone was worth selling her soul. She blushed, thinking about what she'd done in that bed last night while thinking of him. She shook herself and cleared her throat. "I can use some of the cash Luce gave me to get a room. I should leave." He ignored her and began dishing out plates of food. "Jack, did you hear me?"

"Yes, I did. I'm not acknowledging it as a viable option. You're settled." He turned to her. "You didn't like the tub? The bed? Tell me, Rose. Why is accepting help from me so repugnant to you?" There it was. That flash of irritation, and a slip in the accent.

"Bikers don't housesit, and they certainly don't use the word repugnant."

"Well, they do now. And I wasn't always a biker. I inherited the bike."

"Nice inheritance. An adventurous, old uncle?"

"No, it was left to me by my younger brother." He looked up and her face was stricken. "It happened about a year ago."

"I'm sorry, Jack." She let that hang, waiting for him to tell her more, but he didn't. He just slid the plate in front of her and smiled. "You'll like it. Butter chicken, basmati rice, and naan that makes the angels sing."

He wasn't going to tell her, and she could hardly blame him. To lose a sibling so young often meant something had gone terribly wrong. Her experience in the emergency room had proven that.

CHAPTER 4

*R*ose followed Jack out of the townhome, feeling a bit confused and out of sorts. She didn't have a whole lot of experience with men, but she had experience dodging advances. He'd almost kissed her. And when she thought about that, for the first time in a long time, she hadn't wanted to dodge it. Lust had roared through her body. He smelled good, felt even better. Jesus, Joseph, and Mary! This was not a good idea. She couldn't believe she'd told him about Kieran. She walked alongside him, lost in her thoughts until they stopped. Instead of the sensible vehicle he'd driven the night before, he'd brought his Harley. The bike he'd inherited from his brother. She looked up at him.

"As you said, the rain has stopped." He handed her the helmet she'd left strapped to her own bike. "That helmet looks rather retro." It actually had a snap chin strap. It reminded him of those old stunt videos from the eighties, jumping cars with their sparkling helmets. Hers' was the colors of the Irish flag.

"It was my mother's. I found it in my granny's garage."

"You should get a new one. I know that's sentimental, but I'd wager it doesn't pass safety standards."

"Christ, ye look like a thug most of the time. But then ye get this stern look come over you and start talking like a Boy Scout. I can't fathom you, Jack." *But you like Boy Scouts. You love superheroes. And he's a handsome devil.* She blocked out her inner voice, even though it was spot on. She really did like the superhero type. Her bad boy daddy issues truly had been put to rest when she was still a teenager. She liked strong alphas, but she liked them to live clean and with purpose. So she reminded herself for the hundredth time that she'd met him in a biker bar, chock full of ne'r do wells and flat out criminals. She took the seat behind him, and for once, it didn't scratch to ride instead of drive. She liked being in control. Liked having her own bike. But there was something rather delicious about straddling this big bike and taking his hips between her thighs. He smelled clean and masculine, and his leather jacket was well worn and tight over his shoulders. "Put your arms around my waist, love. I know you're not used to riding pillion, but just hold on and keep balanced. Let me steer."

"I know how to ride bitch, Jack. Is pillion one of those big Cambridge words?" She thought she heard him curse under his breath. Then a slight chuckle.

"You're no bitch, Rose, and I've never liked the term. It's as bad as old lady."

"A feminist, male biker. Be still my heart." He really laughed at that, lifting his chin to release a full belly of laughter. It was a beautiful sound.

Rose relaxed as they rode through the small streets of Convent Garden. The architecture was old, and there was a large marketplace. Beautiful glass archways where they couldn't take the bike, but that she longed to walk through. Shops and vendors and overloaded flower containers, lush from the rain of early summer. The sun was peeking out, a rare treat for these parts, and she put her face up to it, wishing she could shed her helmet. She lifted the face shield of her old helmet. It was scarred and scratched from decades of use. She couldn't keep the smile off her face.

Jack loved this feeling. Whipping wind and the hum of the bike under him. The soft, lovely woman behind him. She liked it too. Whether it was the change in weather, the sites, or the company, he didn't know. "We've got a bit of time. You don't have to be in for over an hour. Let's stop and have a look around." He pulled over, finding a motorbike parking area. Much easier to locate than a spot for a car. She dismounted after him and he watched her as she took her helmet off and shook her head. His eyes flared and before he thought better of it, he captured a small lock of her hair between his fingers. "Christ, Rose. You are something to see." She misunderstood, trying to fix her windblown hair. He stopped her hand. "No, love. It's perfect."

Jack wasn't a man prone to losing control, but she looked absolutely breathtaking. Her cheeks were pink from the wind. Her hair looked like she'd had a tussle between the sheets, and he knew if he put his nose to it, that she'd smell like the wind. He wanted to kiss her. Instead, he backed up, releasing that soft, feathery strand of auburn hair. He felt the loss of it like a stab. "Come, let's go get some tea and look around a bit."

"We shouldn't. I should get to work."

"We have time. And that is not your work. Your work is back in Ireland. You're a nurse, Rose. The sooner you get back to that, the safer you'll be." He softened his tone and his words. "And for now, consider yourself kidnapped. You're mine until we pull into Luce's. Are you telling me you aren't interested to see what's under those arches?"

I'm interested to see what's under that clothing if you must know, she thought to herself. Then she admonished herself. *You do NOT like bad boys, Rose.* Yet she followed, and she felt a thrill go through her. So in order to quell any potential trouble, she said aloud, "All right. But I'm not yours and this is not a date. I could use some tea and to stretch this leg out a bit." They began walking under the covered marketplace.

"If you say so, Rose. Now, you're down a pair of jeans. Do you need some clothing?"

She rubbed her face, remembering that her good jeans were in shreds. She suddenly wished for her closet back home. "No, I'll get by."

He stopped at a rack of bohemian clothing. "You're a jeans and t-shirt type, I take it? Or was that just for show while you're looking for your father?"

"I don't need any clothes. I've got another pair of jeans and scrubs for sleeping. I won't be here much longer. I need to get back. If my da doesn't show tomorrow night, I'm coming clean with Luce." He turned to her, jaw tight. "Save it, Jack. My brother can't wait. He's in the hospital battling pneumonia. He cannot wait."

"You should go home. Maybe I can look for him." Fuck, he hated himself right now.

"No, I need to travel with him. I need to know he's coming. I can't let him out of my sight once I find him."

"He doesn't know, does he? About your brother?"

She sighed. "Well, he hasn't exactly been checking in now has he?"

He thought a change of subject was due. She was getting irritated and his self-loathing was spoiling his mood as well. "Stop the press. I've found just the thing." He stopped in front of a rack full of blouses. He chose a lovely off-the-shoulder one made of glowing green fabric and detailed with red roses.

"Jack, I don't need…" he cut her off, holding it up against

her. "It's perfect with your fair skin. And the roses," he shook his head. Maybe he didn't want her in it. Not in that club, at least. "You can wear it out sometime. Live a little. That shirt you're wearing was barely dry when you took it out of the laundry. You obviously packed too light. Let me get it for you."

"Thank you, Jack, but no. Come now, and I'll buy you some tea." She walked on, heading for the tea shop, just in time to miss him hand the clerk a fifty-pound note, double what the shirt cost. "Keep the change," he whispered, then made a sign that said *shh* and stuffed the blouse inside his leather jacket.

His heart squeezed as she handed the tea shop clerk three pounds out of her wallet. He knew she was low on funds. He didn't think she was poor, but she was obviously helping out at home with the expenses. He thought about the decadence of his expenditures. He had two houses in one city, for God's sake. Some of it earned, yes. But some of it was inherited and he hadn't done a thing to earn it. He smiled warmly as she handed him a cup of tea. They went about putting cream and sugar in their cups and continued to walk. He watched her, committing to memory what grabbed her interest. She walked right past jewelry stores and designer clothing. Italian shoes and handbags. She didn't even linger for a moment with that longing look that some women got. What caught her eye was the local art and finally a cart of used books. She thumbed through the novels, stopping at a dog-eared copy of *The Hobbit*.

"I've started rereading this from a copy in your friend's library. He has very good taste in books."

"He does. Do you have a lot of books at home?"

She smiled at that. "More books than shelves. I love going to book sales and auctions. The fun of the auction is watching the rich and the dealers battle over the first editions. The dealers never win, of course, but you've got to admire the sport of it."

"I don't think I've ever been to a country auction. They've got a big auction house in London, of course. I sat through one, once. Just out of curiosity more than anything. My father took me. They take the fun out of it, though. There aren't any genuine finds. They've already figured out what everything's worth. I think a country auction would be a bit different."

"Oh, absolutely. I bought an old writing desk at one auction when I was about fifteen. It was old and in rough shape so I only paid a few pounds for it. Needed polished and a hinge replaced. But then I got it home and found a secret compartment in it. It's very Irish. We keep secrets and we're a suspicious lot. Inside the compartment, there was an old will and a mourning brooch. You know, the sort with the black cloth and the lock of hair. It was creepy altogether. I was thrilled, fancying it was haunted. That there might be a ghost attached to it. You know what it's like to be that age. You're past believing in magic. The fairies have all gone away. But that brooch had me up at night for days, scared shitless under my covers. It was exhilarating."

Jack watched her and was captivated. She was as animated as he'd ever seen her. She was a good person. He suddenly wanted to beat Mick Tierney for every disappointment she'd ever suffered. *The fairies have all gone away.* It was a statement about your innocence fading in the harsh light of the real world. With how her life had gone, he was surprised the fairies had stayed around as long as they had. He didn't know about fairies, but he knew about being a kid. His mother had never been one to play with her children, but he did remember his father. Swashbuckling with fake swords and teaching him sea shanties. He'd told him all about doing a float on the aircraft carriers in the Navy.

About what it was like to go from gliding through the sea waters with the dolphins to soaring with the eagles from his cockpit.

Everyone deserved at least one good parent. Rose hadn't had that. He hoped to hell her grandmother was a good substitute.

"And what about your Grandmother? It must have been hard raising two children at her age."

Rose waved a hand dismissively. "She was a young grandmother. She had my mother at eighteen. Young like my parents when they married. Things were different. By the time she took us on, she was only in her forties. Some women nowadays don't even start having children until they're that age." She cocked her head. "She's not perfect. As I've said, she's Irish and they like their secrets. But she's been a good parent. She did the best she could. She was a single mother when she had my mam. A big scandal back in those days, especially for a Catholic. But she didn't care then and she cares even less now."

"She sounds like a strong woman."

"She is. But Kieran's illness has taken a toll. She's in her sixties now. It's wearing her down, the stress of it all."

"And you. It must be wearing on you as well."

She straightened her spine, chin up. And that's when he saw it. She retreated. Pulled away. "We'd better get going. I don't want to be late."

Rose needed to stay focused. This wasn't a date. She turned to go back to where they were parked and she heard him mumble. "And now you've gone again."

She turned too quickly and her hip had a biting pain. The lid popped off her paper cup, filled with tea. "Buggering, fecking hell!" She cursed. Pulling her t-shirt away from her skin.

"Are you burned?" His tone was panicked.

"No! Not really. I just really can't seem to catch a fecking break right now."

"Maybe you need another day off, Rose."

"I don't. Stop pecking at me!" His lips turned up a bit and she bristled. "Are ye laughing at me?"

He put his hands up in defense. "Christ, no. It's just, you're rather gorgeous when you're angry. Forgive me. Are you sure you're not burned?" He took the cup from her and secured the lid. "You'll need to change."

She looked down at her light colored t-shirt with a huge tea stain down the front. "What is it with this bloody country and my wardrobe? I don't have time to go change."

He did smile fully then. "Well, then. It's good that there's a lav right behind me, and that I bought this back at the shop." He pulled the shirt out of his jacket. She looked scandalized. "Rose, I'm no thief. I did pay for it." He was chuckling at the look on her face.

"Do you have some sort of supernatural abilities? First, you make lodgings materialize and now a shirt right when I need it. It reeks of devilry." He raised a brow and she smirked. "All right, give me the bleedin' shirt."

She stopped as she turned toward the lav. "Thank you, Jack." Then she raised up on her toes and kissed him on the cheek. If he'd been a weeping man, he'd have teared up. This woman was going to doom him.

* * *

JACK REGRETTED GIVING her that blouse as soon as she'd walked out of the loo at the market. He was doubly regretting it as he watched her take off her helmet, shake her head, and walk toward the bar entrance. He'd been right. It was gorgeous on her. She was stiff from that crash, and his heart squeezed as he watched her wince while she reached over her head to handle the helmet. The hip was sore, by her own admission, and he noticed she was favoring the other side. When she walked in, some appreciative whistles slowed her even further, a blush coming over her cheeks. Luce's head came up and he had a flash of something travel over his face. "That's enough, lads." He said with a grumble. That eased Jack's hackles a bit, even as Luce took notice that they were arriving together and sent him a dark look.

As Rose walked toward the bar, a hand snatched out to grab her arm and Hammer said, "Slow down sweet thing. You're looking ripe as a peach today."

Rose couldn't turn the full force of her temper on him, because her injured shoulder gave a howl and she showed the pain on her face and a hitch in her breath. Luce got there first. Lucky for Jack, because he was getting ready to pound the fucker for touching her. Not very prudent given he was undercover. Luce hissed, "Get your feckin' hands off her. Can't ye see you've hurt her you goddamn eejit!"

"She's playing with you, Luce. I barely grabbed her. That's what they do. They play." He sneered.

"I'm fine!" she interjected. "And keep yer hands to yourself! I'm not on the menu." His eyes flared, and Jack saw it. Hammer liked resistance. He liked fire in a woman, or more specifically, liked to snuff it out.

"Says who?" Hammer asked with a lurid gaze.

Jack and Luce spoke in unison. "Says me."

She bristled. "Says me. I'm the only one who gets a say! Now you Neanderthals can go back to your pints and cool off." That's when Luce froze. Rose followed his gaze to her shoulder. The bruising was dark and fresh.

He pulled the blouse elastic down just a bit more and the rage boiled in him to the point of shaking. "Who in the bloody hell put these bruises on you?"

The protectiveness surprised Jack, but he couldn't say it

displeased him. He couldn't be here all the time, and Luce's protective streak might keep her safe from Hammer or anyone else who decided to give her trouble. Then Luce turned on him. "Did you put your fucking hands on her? I saw you come in together!" He advanced on Jack, ignoring Rose's protests. Jack went nose to nose with him.

"She crashed on her bike, Luce. I would never hurt her or any other woman, so back the fuck down."

Luce's eyes narrowed, seeking the truth. "It's true. I'm fine. I'm just a bit sore and bruised."

Jack couldn't help getting one shot in. He was pissed off about this whole thing. About Hammer grabbing her and about Luce accusing him. "It was raining like hell last night, and you just let her leave on that death trap with bald tires. If you want to blame someone, take your own share of it, Luce."

Luce tensed, and Jack thought he was going to hit him. Then his shoulders loosened, and he turned back to Rose. His face softened. "I shouldn't have let you leave in that storm. I didn't think. We take care of our own here. But you should have asked for a ride."

She lifted her chin. "Really, Luce? Who was going to drive me? A drunk or a pervert?" She gave Hammer a scathing look. Luce turned a side eye to him.

"He'll not touch you again, or I'll hear of it." Then he looked her over again. "How did you get here? What about the bike?"

"I brought her," Jack said.

He turned to Jack. "In my office." It wasn't a request.

"Luce..." Rose's irritation was obvious.

He turned to Rose and his face softened again. "Where else are ye hurt, love?"

"I'm okay."

"That's not what I asked."

"Just the hip and shoulder. My helmet took the brunt of

it. I treated the abrasions and iced it all. I'm fine, Luce, truly. I wouldn't lie about my health."

But Luce had turned his focus to her helmet. A haunted look came over his face. "Where did you get that helmet, Rose?"

"A thrift shop," she lied. "Back home."

He searched her face, swallowing hard. "You need to wear something else. That's been through a crash. It's not sound. I'll get one for you. In the meantime, you're not working today. Sammy will work with Candice tonight. Go home to...Where do you live, exactly? I'll take you."

"I can take her," Jack said smoothly.

"Both of you shut your gobs for a minute and let me make my own decisions. I can work tonight. And I'll buy my own bloody helmet." She didn't like taking charity from Luce. Didn't want to owe him.

Luce looked from Jack to her. "Ye might be in charge most of the time, peahen, but this is my house. My rules. You'll go home with your normal wages. I'll call a lift for you, then you won't have to ride with either of us if you don't want to. I'm sorry more than you can know, sweet lass, that I let you drive home in that storm." He brushed a hand over her hair, reverently. "Sammy, call a cab for her." Then he turned back to Jack. "And you, in my office." He turned to Hammer next. "I'll deal with you later. Don't you have some business you're supposed to be doing?"

Hammer sighed, lifting his ass off the stool.

Luce shut the door and strolled by Jack, opening a drawer in his desk and pulling out a bottle of Jameson. He poured a glass and took a shot. Then motioned for Jack to sit. Jack knew what went on in this office after hours, and hoped to God the seat was clean. "Now. Why don't you tell me what the fuck happened last night?"

"She wouldn't take a ride from me. I offered earlier in the

night. I figured I'd follow her, make sure she was okay. I watched her go down when some asshole slid through the intersection."

"Is that when you picked her up?" Jack stayed silent, assessing the man. "Do you need me to repeat the feckin' question?"

"No, I heard you. I'm just not sure if you need all of the details. She's okay. I made sure of it. I have her bike in the shop, which she didn't like but she doesn't really get a say at this point. She needs new tires if she's going to ride in foul weather."

"Are you involved with her, Jackknife?" he asked, eyes narrowed.

"Again, not your concern. There's no need worrying over me. You need to worry about Hammer. He's not the full shilling. I've known men like him before. I don't like the way he watches her. Bring him to heel or I will." Jack knew he was risking being kicked out of the club, but a show of backbone might just get him further into the fold.

"Who the bloody fuck do you think yer talking to? This is my house." Luce leaned over the desk, menace rolling off him.

"Yes, Luce. And in your house, she's at your mercy for protection. I'm not trying to piss you off, for fuck's sake. I'm trying to keep Rose safe. She's made a cock-up of doing it herself. Do you have any idea what it was like watching that car skid toward her? Watching her lay that bike down? I'm not the problem here!"

Luce shut his eyes at the thought. Then he shook himself. "I'll look after her. Where is she living? I don't know enough about her."

"She's been moved. I'll save you the tale about where she was sleeping. It would just get your blood up again. She's somewhere safer now, but she's entitled to her privacy. You aren't getting anything else out of me. It's her call. And if that means you toss me out, then so be it."

Luce stared at him, not speaking. He finally exhaled. "Okay. Fair enough. Now, let's get you a drink. I think we both need one."

Jack got up and went for the door. "Jackknife." Jack turned silently. "I'm glad you were there."

Jack said, "So am I. If I had any sort of say in the matter, which I don't, she'd be back in that little town in Ireland and far away from this place."

Luce called out to the main bar. "Sammy, get this man a glass of my best whiskey. Hammer, in my office!"

They'd been in the office for about ten minutes when Jack took a stroll to the public lav. It was next to Luce's office. He went into the nasty, one-hole piss pot and locked the door. Then he went to the vent, took out his contraband phone, and hit digital record. His work phone had a great mic on it, but it might not be good enough. He wasn't sure if it would pick up the sound, but it was worth a try. He heard them talking. Arguing, actually. He caught part of it, but he couldn't be sure. When he heard Hammer leave and slam the door, he kept the recording on, hearing Luce make a phone call. Then it was done. He stowed his phone after shutting it off and went out to have another drink. Luce was right. He did need it.

CHAPTER 5

The clubhouse was hopping at Noon as Rose arrived on her motorcycle behind Jack. They'd put a tent up coming out the back entrance because other chapters had come in for the party. She looked around frantically, trying to find the dark hair and dark eyes that would be her father twenty years older.

Jack's gut turned as he watched Rose because he knew that she was looking for her father. She wasn't going to find him, but he'd needed to stall her. He didn't want her telling Luce who she was. He wondered as he watched Luce's face focus on her if he already knew. An old hurt seemed to surface in his eyes. After all, he'd been friends with Mick Tierney all this time. And he was Irish like Annalise. He'd bet his ass that Annalise had been how the two men met. Did Rose look like her mother? She had her father's eyes, but the rest was nothing like him. Fair skin, auburn hair, and delicate features.

"Rose! Come over here, lass!" Rose walked over to Luce and realized he was already slightly intoxicated. More relaxed than she'd ever seen him. "How are ye, girl? I told you to take a couple of days!"

She smiled, "Well, now. I didn't want to miss the party. You're so old, ye might very well drop dead before I come into work next shift."

Luce threw back his head and laughed. "Well, now. Just for that, ye've got to give me a gift."

She cocked her head and he pointed. There was a small stage, microphones, and a few men tuning instruments.

She put her hands up and said, "Oh no you don't."

"Aye, I do. Searched high and low for a band to do a traditional session. You did say you were a musician. Was that a load of bollocks or are you going to live up to your bloodline, woman?"

"Cheeky bastard," she mumbled. "Maybe a little later, but only one song, Luce."

"Five," he said with a grin.

"Two."

"Three." She sighed and he knew he'd won.

"Okay, three. But I pick the songs." She pointed at him, eyes narrowed.

Jack watched the interaction with amusement. Sometimes he had to remind himself this was a serious job. Had to prick his conscience with a reminder about his brother. Because the truth was, that these guys knew how to party. How many young men and women had been enticed by this do or die mentality? They lived hard and fast. But it wasn't just that. If it was, Jack wouldn't be here. The underbelly of this society was steeped in organized crime. At this very moment, the digital recording was being sharpened and deciphered at MI5 headquarters. The conversation he'd recorded between Hammer and Luce could very well have been about their search for Mick Tierney. They suspected he was either dead or had been arrested. The phone conversation had been harder to make out, mainly because it was one-sided. It was some sort of deal. Whether it was drugs or guns, he didn't yet know.

"You look too serious, Jackknife. Pull up a chair and Candice will bring you a drink. Candice!" Luce yelled over his shoulder. Candice brought them both a pint of stout. "No bitter tonight, lad. Good Irish stout!" A few of the men whooped and he noticed their patches were from an Irish chapter.

An hour later, the band was in full swing and there were leather-clad drunkards stomping their feet and playing grab ass with the club women. Other men had their women with them, and even a few kids. Like a big family reunion full of thugs and repeat offenders. Still, they were tight. They seemed to take care of their own. The only problem with that was the collateral damage. His brother had likely been nothing to them. No loss. Annalise Tierney had been another casualty, and her children had grown up without a mother or a father. Could someone here really have beaten and strangled her? Shot her in the head and thrown her in the river? He looked at Rose, and his chest ached. His body twitched with protective instincts. He sipped his Guinness and slowed his breathing as he looked around. That's when he saw Hammer. He had one of the other girls on his lap. She was obviously high. She'd have to be to keep her kippers down while sitting in that mutant's lap. Hammer shoved his hand in the low neckline of her shirt and she winced as he pinched her. His hands explored her, but his eyes were fixed to the right. On Rose. He let out a low growl, and Luce looked up sharply.

"You really don't like Hammer." It wasn't a question. "Aye, well. He is a bit of a rabid dog, but even dogs have their purpose."

"The only thing a rabid dog needs is to be caged or put

down. Better you should have a working dog. Focused and disciplined."

"Are you applying for the job, Jackknife? Because no offense intended, but ye don't seem the sort to prospect. Bottom of the food chain doesn't seem yer style, and you have to work to be where Hammer is."

"I'll pass if it means licking his ass. I'm surprised your second isn't a little more brains and less brawn." Jack said, probing.

"He didn't want the job," Luce mumbled. And Jack wondered if he was referring to Mick. There was a stir toward the music area, and his breath caught in his throat as he watched Rose take the stage. The men all whooped and he watched Luce's face transform. He suddenly wanted to throw blinders on every man in attendance.

"Well, now. This is a grand day altogether. What do you say we have a toast to the birthday lad?"

One of the men shouted, "I'll toast, but he's a bit gray for a lad!"

"Young enough to kick your ass, brother!" Luce shot back with a grin. The crowd roared. Rose had been speaking with the band earlier, getting her three tunes together. They had numerous instruments with them, switching off depending on the tune. Rose borrowed a violin and a bow, and Jack's heart leaped like a boy's in his chest.

She said. "This first song is a warning to all you younger lads. Beware of conniving, strong-minded, Irish women. Not everyone can handle us."

"I could handle you! Come sit over here!" Someone shouted.

Luce bellowed. "Shut your gob, Englishman. And pay attention!" They started and Luce let out a laugh. He raised a brow. *"Wearin' the Britches,"* he said, recognizing the Irish folk song.

73

*Come all young men where e'er you be and listen to me
lamentation
I courted a girl beyond compare and I loved her with admiration
At length in time she became my wife, t'was not for beauty but for
riches
And all the time it causes strife, to see which of us will wear the
britches*

HER VOICE WAS high and clear, and Jack watched her with complete focus, forgetting why he was here. Forgetting everything but her. The amusing tune continued, and if he wasn't half in love with her already, she took the opportunity during a break in the song to draw that bow across her fiddle and join in with the other musicians. Suddenly, grown grizzly bears were stomping their feet and a few were even swinging their women around. He broke away from his focus for a moment, looking next to him. Luce was as still as the dead, enthralled, eyes shining. It made Jack want to throw him down on the ground and beat him half to death. She was not for the likes of him or any other man here. *Mine,* his inner barbarian growled. *She's mine.* He was utterly and completely fucked.

She finished the tune and they were all on their feet. A blush had spread over her face, and he warmed as her eyes found him, a shy smile forming on her face. He shouldn't be so stupidly pleased over it, but he was. Then Luce spoke. "That was fine, lass. Like the old days. Now let's have another. Something sad and sweet."

She cleared her throat and said, "Yes, I suppose it's not a proper session without murder, mayhem, or melancholy. Sad and sweet it is."

When they started, Jack watched the haunting tune wash

over Luce. An old hurt, perhaps. Her voice was so beautiful. So sweet and sad.

> *Oh the bride and bride party to church they did go*
> *The bride she rode foremost for to make the best show*
> *And I followed after my heart full with woe*
> *For to see my love wed to another*
> *Oh the first time I saw her it was in the church stand*
> *A ring on her finger and her love by the hand*
> *And says I my wee lassie sure I'll be your man*
> *Although you are wed to another*

LUCE CLOSED his eyes like he'd been struck, and that's when the idea sparked in Jack's mind. Jesus! That was it. Annalise, Rose's mother. Had he loved her? They were both from Belfast. He was a little older, but the way he looked at Rose, it was possible. Had there been a love triangle? Had he killed Rose's mother in a fit of jealousy? Mick had an alibi, but maybe he'd done it and the brother-in-law had lied for him? Not likely. A blood brother, maybe, but a copper giving a fake murder alibi for his misguided in-law seemed less likely. He needed to call Katherine. Needed to probe into the relationship between the two men and Annalise Tierney. This might be their in with Mick. Something to finally get him to turn on Luce.

* * *

ROSE LEFT EARLY, bowing out of the party soon after her third song. Her da hadn't shown, and for the first time since this whole thing had started, she was worried. She knew he had a sister, but she didn't know much else. She remembered her aunt in small glimpses, but nothing about where she lived or even her last name. If she could find her da's extended family, maybe they could all be tested as potential donors. Her brother was AB negative, the rarest blood type, and she figured maybe that's why it had been so difficult to match him for marrow or stem cells. It was the HLA cheek swab that actually screened donors, not blood, but there seemed to be some sort of odds stacked against him for finding a match. All she could do was hope that someone on their da's side could help him. Meanwhile, he waited on that damn list, waiting for a miracle. All of her co-workers and fellow nursing students had been swabbed, as well many of their old mates from childhood. Even the people at their church. But there'd been no luck. She called her brother when she got off her bike in front of the townhouse. It went straight to voicemail, so she left a message. She fumbled with her keys, carrying her old helmet and a new one.

When she opened the door to the townhouse, something was off. Like a shift in air current that told her she wasn't alone. She came through the interior door to the kitchen and froze.

"Jackson, where the hell have you been! You didn't answer your..." The young woman's voice trailed off as her jaw dropped. She took a step back and grabbed the paring knife off the counter. "Who the bloody hell are you?"

Rose stepped back as well; hands splayed up in as non-threatening a gesture as she could make. Jesus, was this a girlfriend? "I'm sorry. I think there's been a mistake. How about you put that knife down and we'll get this sorted."

"Where is my brother?" The girl showed some backbone, which Rose admired. She also felt a wave of relief wash over her.

"You must be his sister, the dancer. Amelia, was it? My

76

name is Rose Tierney." That seemed to take some of the tension from the girl's demeanor. "I'm so sorry. Obviously, Jack didn't tell you I was staying here. I didn't mean to scare you. Would you like me to go until you can get hold of Jack?"

"You're Irish?" The girl's curiosity was coming to the forefront. "You're not his usual type." That made Rose bristle until she followed up with, "Oh, that wasn't an insult. The women he usually dallies with are a bit more cold and uptight. So, Rose. I was just cutting a bit of salad. Why don't you join me and tell me what on earth my brother has been up to."

AFTER TWO HOURS, Rose felt like she'd known Amelia all her life. She noticed a limp, and the young woman's foot was in an air cast. The nurse in her had to pry. Stress fractures. Bad ones. Not surprising given the ballet career, but she knew it could be a career ender. She kept that to herself. She was also painfully thin. She ate the salad with no dressing other than vinegar. She'd chopped carrots and kept them on the side, only adding them to Rose's bowl. Same with the cheese. All that effort to end up still getting injured. Rose was suddenly glad that scrubs came in many sizes, and were roomy. She could have all the cheese she wanted and still be a nurse.

They'd gone from talking about school, to their hometowns, and eventually into more private matters that women always seemed to confide over. She'd avoided talking too much about Jack, other than to tell her briefly why she'd ended up here. She left the part out about her crash and where she'd really met Jack. His sister seemed like a straight arrow. Very driven. And she probably didn't know about the company Jack kept on a daily basis. It wasn't her place to tell her.

"My first kiss." Amelia smiled. "Blake Covington in the third year of primary school. His parents were American diplomats and he had a Spiderman knapsack." Rose smiled at that. "And yours?"

"Johnny Murphy in my sixth year. Late bloomer, obviously. He was seventh year and very tall. I had to get on my toes to seal the deal."

"Okay, first lover." Amelia's eyes sparkled with mischief.

Rose tensed, "You first."

She laughed and said, "Fair enough. He was a mate of mine, really. I just got tired of it all. I was the only girl I knew that hadn't done it. He had more experience. He'd done it twice. So, we split a bottle of wine and went for it."

"And was it pure magic?" Rose gave her a cheeky, knowing look.

"No, quite the contrary. Completely underwhelming. I winced, he grunted, and that was that. I was lying there sprawled underneath him thinking I missed something. Surely that was just the beginning of things and he was going to get down to it."

Rose was shaking her head laughing. "You poor thing! Did he try again?"

"No, I think he sensed I didn't want an encore. It was rather awkward to be honest. I wonder whatever happened to the poor lad."

"Well, if he didn't get with the program, I'd imagine he's married to a very unfulfilled woman," Rose clinked her glass of milk to Amelia's water glass and she giggled.

"I did meet someone later. Someone I really liked who did the job properly. I was with him for about six months. He couldn't take my dance schedule or the demands of my work. It's very consuming. He lives in Yorkshire now, probably engaged to some woman with a little more time to be a proper partner to him. I don't blame him, really. He was a good guy." She waved her hand dismissively. "Okay, Rose. Your turn. Let's hear it." Amelia's smile faded as she saw Rose's face lose some of its light. "Oh, Rose. I'm sorry. I shouldn't be so nosey. You don't have to…"

"It's okay. I don't mind. Turnabout is fair play. His name was Owen. He was a bit older. I was singing in a pub for extra money, between the time I finished secondary school and was going to start my studies for nursing school. I hadn't even turned eighteen yet. He worked at the pub, and he was always payin' attention to me. I thought it was exciting, him being older and all that. I let him take me out a couple of times. When we got down to it, I was a bit unsure. He took me to his one-room flat. He only had a pull-out couch. And I thought, you know, that we'd ease into it. I mean, my friends talked about all this foreplay shite and I was expecting a lot more than I got. He pulled my knickers off and just went for it."

Amelia winced, "Did you tell him to slow down? What a bastard."

"Aye, I tried. He didn't hear me or didn't care. It was really starting to hurt. You know, like tearing. I wasn't ready. I tried to push him off, and he just shoved into my body and told me there was no goin' back now. I shut my eyes and let him do his thing. Then he got off me and it was done. He didn't hold me or anything. Seemed a bit put out, actually. He said men didn't like to stop once they got started and that I had a lot to learn. I just told him to fuck off, put my pants on, and I left him standing there with his condom still on. I quit the pub after that."

"I'm sorry Rose. I'm sorry that happened to you. So when did you find someone to take your virginity the right way? Do you have a man back in Ireland? You said you weren't seeing my brother. Who's the man that finally treated you right?"

"There's been no one. There is no one. That was my only time. It kind of put me off the whole business, honestly. I mean, if that's all there is to it, then why bother? Some women like it, but they're obviously finding better men than I did. And I'm very busy. Working and going to school. It just seemed better to go it alone."

"Well, if you aren't seeing anyone, maybe it's time to give it another go. My brother is single. And you can't fault his taste in real estate. I mean, did you see that tub? He's really got a knack for house buying. His other home in Battersea is just as nice. More modern. Nothing like the stuffy manse where we grew up. What's wrong, Rose? What did I say?"

Rose realized her mouth was open and her brow was turned in. "Nothing at all. I just remembered I forgot my sunglasses at work," she lied. "I left my sunglasses, and it just popped into my head."

"Do you need them tonight?"

"No, and they're cheap. Not a big deal. Sorry, do go on. Tell me about the place in Battersea? I haven't heard of that neighborhood. It sounds like your brother has it all."

Amelia told her, but she barely heard the words. Rose was seething. Jesus, she was so stupid. *Housesitting my ass.* He not only came from money, but he'd lied to her about owning the house. What else was he lying about? How could she have trusted someone she didn't even know?

"Well, it's been very nice getting to know you. I'll get out of your hair. I took the tube, so I guess I'll head over to the other flat and see if I find him there. He works a lot, so he might be pulling an all-nighter. I have keys."

"You don't have to take the tube. I'll drive you over. You can show me the flat. If he's there, maybe we can all go out for a drink. You can wear my new helmet and I'll wear my old one." Bullshit. She was going to check out his other home and figure out who the hell Jackson De Clare was. Even his name sounded posh. What she knew for certain was that he was not some random biker, and she'd had enough of secrets.

* * *

ROSE HAD NEVER HAD a passenger on her bike other than her brother when he was younger. He was too big to ride with her now. Amelia squealed as Rose revved the engine. The new tires and the tune up made all the difference. But she pushed that thought aside. The bastard hadn't cashed in a favor. He'd probably paid for it. A few hundred pounds to the mechanics was probably nothing to him. Her face flushed with anger. "Your brother never takes you on his bike?"

Amelia barked out a laugh. "Not bloody likely. My mother would have a stroke. They treat me like a china doll. All of them do…or did. My father and Louie are gone, as you know. Which only made the protective streak worse with Jackson."

She thought about the sensible Peugeot station wagon he'd been driving. He'd gone to a lot of trouble to appear as something he wasn't. Why would a blue blood from Chelsea be slumming it with Luce and his club boys? As they pulled into the parking area near the Thames, she looked up at the large warehouse that had been converted into luxury apartments.

"Come on up. His bike isn't here and…" Amelia stopped, looking at the station wagon. "Why is Judith's Peugeot parked here?"

Rose clenched her jaw. She said lightly, "Who's Judith?"

Amelia answered, "My mother's cook."

Rose swore under her breath. Of course they had a cook. Probably at the manse, for feck sake. She was going to wring Jack's neck. "I'll park in the overflow parking. I don't want to take his spot. I'll meet you at the front. You shouldn't walk that far. Ye need to get off your feet."

The flat was awe inspiring. The view of the Thames was top notch. "Help yourself to a drink if you like. I need a bath. His spa tub is calling my name. I need to soak this." She motioned to her foot.

"Do you want me to head off?" Rose said, hoping she said no.

"No way. I'll only be about a half hour. Then we can raid his wine cabinet." She winked.

She left Rose and went to the main suite. Rose had wanted to check out his closet. People hid a lot in their closets. Instead she headed to his office. She made quick work of the search. Bills, bank statements. She didn't look too closely at those, because she felt a little like a letch for doing this. He had lied, a lot, but he'd also taken her in, tried to protect her from Hammer, fixed her bike. She looked discretely through the drawers. Then she'd found something odd. A small safe that looked too insignificant to hold much. It was bolted under the desk and it was open. She slid her hand in and felt around. The item she pulled out was, in hindsight, not a surprise. An empty handgun magazine. It was his pistol safe. There was also a wallet. He carried a different wallet on him. She'd seen it attached to a chain in his pocket. A lot of bikers had them, so it didn't fall out of their pocket as they rode. He always paid cash at the pub. This one was different. She opened the slim leather wallet and her blood pressure spiked. *Agent Jackson De Clare.* It contained MI5 credentials. Holy God. He was a feckin' superhero. Alter-ego and all.

CHAPTER 6

*J*ack dismounted his bike in the dark, parking in his usual spot. He'd managed to escape the party after nursing a couple of pints. He didn't like driving his bike with a buzz. It was dangerous. And he didn't fancy passing out under the billiards table as Sammy had done. There were so many people there; no one would miss him. What he'd really wanted to do was follow Rose out of there, go back to the townhouse, and tell her everything. Then, if she'd have him, he would have laid her out in front of that big hearth and rogered her until neither of them could move. This was killing him. Watching her on that stage was a sort of torture. She was remarkable. Talented, smart, and absolutely lovely. And she was a nurse. An honorable profession. And given her parentage, that was saying something about her internal core. She had a bit of a wild streak, probably from her father. The temper, however, was all Irish.

Watching her look around that party for her father had been agonizing. Something had to give. She wasn't a criminal, and it was time to come clean with her. Take her to her father. They were stalled on this case. On a good note, he'd heard back from Katherine. They'd cleaned up the recording. Something was going down soon. He wondered if all of the chapters meeting for Luce's birthday had a dual purpose. That aside, he'd go to Rose tomorrow. He would sit her down and make her understand. Then he'd see if she could talk some sense into her father. They'd be getting the tissue and blood sample results back tomorrow or the next day. He prayed to God the father was a match. He'd read up on the matching process. HLA matching was more precise than blood typing and matching. Sometimes a total stranger was a better match than a family member. That's why he'd decided he was going to get himself tested. It was the least he could do, and it was anonymous. The agency never needed to know. He was breaking all sorts of rules for Rose. One more wasn't going to matter.

He walked into the flat and heard giggling. His sister's distinct, tinkling laugh that made him think of woodland sprites. He warmed at the sound. "Jackson! It's about time you showed yourself. We've opened a bottle of obscenely expensive French wine." He came around the wall that separated the foyer, with its security cameras and motion sensors, to the open space of the sprawling flat. And froze. His sister stood with a glass of his good claret, and next to her was Rose. *Buggering hell.*

Rose watched Amelia gimp over at a surprisingly fast pace and leap into her brother's arms. He enveloped her and picked her up off her feet. "Hello love. You've hurt yourself."

Well, at least he didn't try to keep up with the fake, East London accent. He obviously knew he was caught on some level. But he was still shocked as he met her eyes and she flashed his credentials. He closed his eyes, as if struck. Then collected himself and kissed his sister on the top of the head. He directed his eyes to Amelia, then shook his head slightly. She understood. Amelia had no idea what he actually did for a living. She tucked the credentials in a drawer in the kitchen, never letting him free of her stare. Then gave one nod. "I'd love to stay and chat, but I just wanted to get your sister delivered.

Jack looked down at Amelia. "You came on the bike?"

Amelia rolled her eyes and gave Rose a conspiratorial look. "See. I've told you how he is. Completely overprotective."

"I've been on the receiving end of that myself. It starts to scratch a bit in large doses. Have fun tonight, and stay off that foot." She breezed by Jack and he caught her arm.

"I'll see you bright and early." His look held regret. "Don't do anything rash." He said the words low, just for her. Amelia had gone to retrieve her wine glass.

"I'm counting on it. Bright and early."

* * *

"I LIKE HER. Explain to me, because I'm a bit slow on the social aspects of being in your late twenties. Why aren't you seeing her romantically?"

"It's complicated."

"I see. Yet you're taking care of her. You've moved her into the townhouse. Is that beard for her?" Her grin was downright devilish.

"It's only for a short time. It was the right thing to do. She needed a place to stay; the house was empty."

Amelia looked at him indulgently. "You've never looked at a woman the way you look at her, Jackson. You run through them regularly. No one has ever put that look on your face."

"I don't have a look."

"You do. You're falling in love with her."

"Don't be daft, Amelia. You're reading too many novels."

The brush-off irritated her, but she knew it was a defense mechanism.

"Jackson, it's okay to care for someone. I really like her. Complications can be overcome. Just be careful with her. She's not as tough as she seems."

"What does that mean?" he asked.

"It means you want her. You've got steam coming off you, you want her so badly. But she and I have bonded quickly. I spent the evening talking with her. She's rather sweet and open if she doesn't feel threatened. Let's just say, she hasn't had a good experience with men."

"If you are referring to her father, I know." Jackson hated this conversation. He needed to change the subject. He had blurred the lines horribly between work and his family.

"I don't know anything about her father other than her granny raised her. I'm talking about men men. She's had a rough start. That's all I'm going to say. Just tread carefully. To be her age, she's rather innocent."

"You are being very cryptic."

"I'm a woman, Jackson. It's what we do."

He moved closer to her on the leather sofa. "No, you're not. You're my little sister. You're supposed to be carrying your doll around and wearing ruffles. Stop this woman nonsense instantly. I'm not ready for it."

She nestled in next to him. "I've missed you, Jackson. I came to you instead of mother's house because I wanted to feel relaxed and appreciated."

"Tell me about your injuries." His tone was grim.

"Stress fractures in my right foot. Two of them. They're bad. I thought they'd healed, but these new routines for the audition have a lot of point. A lot of stress on my right foot. It just gave way." She started to tear up in silence. "Mother will be so disappointed."

"Don't you dare put that on yourself. Mother was born

disappointed. Your health is the concern here. What do you want to do, love? Do you really want this career if it's going to take this sort of toll on your body? You're the thinnest I've ever seen you."

"I thought if I lost more weight, and just took calcium supplements, the strain wouldn't be as bad. It's what my teacher suggested."

"Remind me to pound that motherfucker into the studio mirror next time I see him." His sister tensed, surprised at her well-mannered brother's language. "Sorry."

"Well, now. A crack in the armor. Good for you, Jackson. Or Jack. That's what Rose calls you. You never said anything. Do you prefer Jack?"

"It doesn't matter what you call me. Just stay safe. Just come see me more often." He pulled her closer.

"That street goes both ways. Do you think I could stay with you? I don't want to stay near the campus. My roommate is going to be practicing, and heading to rehearsal and I'm on the bench, so to speak. It's too depressing. I can take the tube."

"You'll take the Jag. As soon as I switch with Judith again. We'll go tomorrow afternoon."

"I don't even want to know why on earth you switched cars with Judith. Although, she's likely the talk of the town with her friends seeing her roll up in a new Jaguar."

He just chuckled against his sister's fair hair. He wanted to scoop her up and get in a time machine. He wanted to go back in time to the age of twelve. Watching her in her first years of ballet as a toddler, when it was still fun and didn't hurt. "I love you, sister."

"I love you too, Jack. Now, no offense, but you need to get the hell out of here." He leaned back to look her in the eye. "You can't let her stew all night. Whatever you did, go now and fix it. And then turn on the charm, dear brother. She's

87

not just going to fall over with her legs in the air like they usually do."

He choked and then started to laugh. "I am so not ready for you to be all grown up."

* * *

JACK DIDN'T BOTHER with pretenses. He slid the key in the door and walked in, surprised to see the lights off. The fire was going, and he melted in his boots when he saw her asleep in his big chair. She looked small and child-like. She was beautiful, her hair aflame in the light of the fire. He tread softly, sat in the chair across from her, and waited.

Rose felt him before she opened her eyes. He didn't make a sound, but the air had changed. She could smell leather and shaving products, feel his warm presence. He'd done a sneak attack, obviously hoping she'd be too sedated to give him a proper lashing. *Think again.*

She didn't even open her eyes. "Start telling me the truth right now, or I swear to Christ I will tell Luce who you are."

She opened her eyes, ready. Or so she thought. The beauty of him still hit her in the belly. He was silent and still. His eyes unapologetically watching her. His face was tender, which she hadn't expected. Her only defense was to stay angry. She shot out of the chair.

"I knew you were a London chancer. You might have good pedigree and a badge, but you are a feckin' snake and a liar all the same." His face shifted to anger. He stood, advancing on her.

"I'm sorry, Rose. Do I disappoint? I've got an honorable goddamn profession instead of being some leather-clad reprobate?"

"Another Cambridge word? Jesus, you are something else.

Well, at least you've settled on an accent. Don't slip up while you're at the club, me Lord."

"Stop it."

"Oh, I'm sorry. Is it Earl de Clare? Viscount? Some other sort of silver spoon bullshit!"

"I won't apologize for my background. It is beside the point. I'm doing a job, Rose. An important one."

"Investigating two-bit thugs at a biker bar?"

"You have no bloody idea what those men are involved in. You should go back to Ireland tomorrow morning. I'll book the ferry ticket myself. Or I'll arrange to get your bike delivered, and you can fly. Just go, Rose. Forget you ever came here."

"I can't! I need to find my da!" Then she stopped short, taking in his shift of expression. "Oh my God. You've been hanging out there for weeks. Do you know my father?" When he didn't answer, she got in close and pushed him. "Answer me!"

"Not formally, no." His tone was flat.

"Where is my father? Jesus, Jack. You knew I needed to find him. Are you really that much of a cold bastard? You've been playing the caring gentleman, but you really don't give a hang about me, do you?"

His temper finally flared. He grabbed her by the elbows. "Are you serious? Do you know how many bleeding rules I've broken for you? Do you know the lengths I've gone to and lines I've crossed to keep you safe?"

She didn't understand. He let her go. "It doesn't matter. I was going to come clean anyway. I'd already decided. You aren't involved in any of the criminal activity and the sooner you are quit of this whole thing the better. They've had your father in custody. We already sent samples to the hospital in Belfast. We should have the results today."

She shook her head, not grasping what she was hearing.

"You've had him this whole time?" Then she registered what else he'd said. "You had him tested properly?"

"Yes, we took him to a hospital after hours. Gave him the full workup, not just a swab." He looked at her and her chin was trembling. "I hope he's a match, Rose. I really do. Despite who he is, your brother is innocent. So are you. I wish I could take this all away for you, but I've done all I can."

"Why are you holding him? What has he done?" she asked.

"As far as I can tell, he's the cleanest of the bunch. He's an enforcer within the club. Kind of the den mother that makes sure the boys are following orders and staying in line with the club rules."

"I didn't know they had any," she said wryly.

"Don't be fooled into thinking these boys are just party animals with motorcycles. They have a hierarchy. They are deep into all sorts of organized crime. Drugs, prostitution, and guns. The unholy trinity of their doctrine."

"Why you? Why were you put undercover with them? You don't seem the sort to be assigned to this sort of work. You seem like you'd be more comfortable in a suit and tie. It never really fit."

He measured her for a moment, deciding how much to tell her. "My brother overdosed outside their club. They were selling him heroin laced with fentanyl. I forced the issue. I threatened to quit if they didn't give me this case."

"Well, I suppose you wouldn't be doing it for the salary." *A bloody Boy Scout. Just her brand of superhero. Dammit!* "Take me to my father. Now." Her voice was harsh again. She was not going to bond with him over losing a sibling. She had to concentrate on her own problems.

"I'll have to arrange it. My superiors may not agree. All I can do is try. Perhaps you can talk some sense into him. He hasn't given up anything on the club. Although, that may change when he sees you. There's a lot I need to tell you. I will tell you what I can. But trust me when I tell you that I am a low ranking agent, and they don't have to do anything. I may lose my job altogether. They don't know I've been housing you. It was completely unprofessional. I am hip deep in broken rules at this point."

That made her stop short. "Why?"

"You really don't know, Rose?" His eyes took in her face, and she felt like he'd caressed her with his hands.

"Why?" she repeated.

He didn't answer her. He just closed the distance between them and said. "I'm sorry."

"For what?" she asked.

"For this," he said hoarsely, and then he kissed her.

CHAPTER 7

*J*ack took her mouth, and the taste of her shot straight to his groin. He moaned as she softened for him, letting him in. "Rose," her name was a desperate whisper, and she gave him her mouth again. He tangled his hands in her hair, as he'd dreamed of doing. "What are you doing to me? Jesus, Rose. I need this." He kissed her deeper, his tongue sliding silkily against hers. He knew he had to stop, but it was going to kill him. *Just a little more.* He slid his hand to her lower back and pressed her to him, and she put her arms around his neck, pulling him closer, grazing his scalp with her nails.

Rose was lost. She was being consumed and she couldn't pull away for anything. His thick arousal was pressed against her belly. She'd always wanted him. What had kept her back were the secrets and the misconception that he was like the other men in that club. She'd known something wasn't right, just as he'd sensed it with her. So, now that she knew he was a liar, why the hell did she have her tongue in his mouth? She was achingly aroused. She'd never felt this kind of passion. Why did he have to be so damn beautiful? Why couldn't he have been a completely ordinary biker shitbird. She could have resisted that.

He pulled away abruptly. "I'm sorry. I can't do this. We have to stop, Rose. This isn't fair to you." He backed up, running his hands through his shaggy hair. She thought about that ID with his picture. Short hair, clean shaven, a suit and tie that probably cost more than her bike.

"You're right. We can't. I'll get my things and go. I'll find a hostel," she said tightly.

"You aren't leaving, Rose."

She gave him a sharp look. "You need to get back to your life. I need to see my da and then go back to Ireland. I'll keep going to work for the next few days. They'll suspect something if I disappear."

"I don't want you there, Rose. It's not safe. You don't know everything. I need to tell you everything before you see your father. Please, sit. I promise I won't touch you. It's my problem, this attraction. I won't apologize for wanting you, Rose, but I won't act on it."

She grinned at the thought. Did he really think that kiss was going to be enough? She was painfully aroused and that had been one hell of a kiss. This was pure dynamite between them. Then he started to talk, and the bottom dropped out of her world.

Jack watched as the details about her mother sank in. Then she started to tremble. She was so pale. He stood, then knelt before her. "Rose, darling. I'm sorry. I didn't know it all at first. The information has been trickling in and it's still a cold case. I'm so sorry. But it's occurred to me that this has something to do with your memory loss."

She had her arms wrapped around herself like she was cold. Physical shock. "I don't understand? What do you mean?" Her eyes searched his and widened. "Oh, God. You think I saw something? When I was a little girl? You think I saw her murdered?"

"I don't know, Rose. I just know that this sort of memory loss is usually trauma induced. I remember a lot of my life from the age of four to six and a half. You only remember glimpses and your mother seems to have been completely erased. Emotional trauma fits." Her tears broke his heart. He pulled her off the chair and took her in his lap and she wept. She'd been told the lie for so long. That her mother had accidentally drowned in the river. He'd spare her the reality if he could, but she was in danger. If Annalise Tierney's murderer was among the ranks of the Sons of the Fallen, then her memory could get triggered at any time. She was safer if she knew the truth.

Rose wept until she shook with it. Her eyes closed tight, she ran through the pictures inside the photo albums in Granny's parlor. Every shot of her mother that she'd greedily drank in, trying to remember. Then her mind stopped at one, like a film strip that had paused. She was in her mother's lap in front of a cake. There were two candles on the cake, a 2 and a 6. It was her mother's birthday. Rose was in her lap so she could help blow out the candles. Her father had taken the picture, she assumed. Her mother was pregnant with Kieran and Rose was five years old. Suddenly the snapshot seemed to have life breathed into it. She felt her mother's arms. Smelled shampoo and body lotion. Felt her hair tickle her cheek. She looked up at her mother through a child's eyes. *Happy Birthday, Mammy.* Then her mother kissed her between the eyes. After all this time, she'd finally found her mother. Like a heavy rain after a long draught, the memory nourished and drowned her all at once. She sobbed in Jack's arms. "Oh, Mammy. My mammy."

Jack's tears were silent. He held them in, refusing to let them fall. He'd lost his father as a young man, but he had an entire childhood full of memories. Good memories. His poor, heartbroken Rose had been robbed of it all. So had her brother. If it killed him, he'd find out why. Jack's brother had died at his own hand. Yes, Jack wanted revenge. His brother had been a foolish boy trapped in an overindulged man's body. As much as he'd loved Louie, that was the ugly truth. Annalise Tierney had been a young mother with a new baby and a little girl who loved and needed her. He would avenge that death. There would be a reckoning for what they'd both lost. He whispered the vow, and he knew Rose hadn't heard it. She was lost in a cold lake of her own sorrow.

ROSE WOKE SLOWLY. She vaguely remembered Jack carrying her upstairs. She made her way through the darkness. He'd promised he wouldn't leave her, but he wasn't in the room. She descended the stairs, going to the spare bedroom. The door was open, and he was asleep with a book next to him. The dim reading lamp was still on. She didn't want to be alone. She couldn't bear it. She eased in next to him and curled under his arm. He woke with a start then looked down at her. Her eyes were swollen from sleep and crying.

"I just needed you. I'm sorry. That sounds a bit pathetic, but I can't be alone right now." He said nothing. He just reached for the lamp, turned it off and pulled her under the covers into the warm shelter of his arms.

They slept a while, but Rose stirred against him, and his cock stirred. He'd cut the thing off before he tried to take advantage of her. He moved his hips away, and she rolled to face him. She arched against him and nuzzled his neck. He felt her tongue taste his skin. "Rose, wake up."

"I'm completely awake," she whispered his name as she kissed him and he was done for. He rolled into her body as she accepted him between her legs. Thankfully, he wore pajama bottoms. She was in sleeping shorts and a soft, thin t-shirt. He ran a hand down to her ass and pulled her into his hard cock. He kissed her deep and slow. Lazily, not wanting to miss a single sensation. He could make this just about her. He could. He didn't need to take her completely. She was looking for comfort and release. He could give her that. "Darling Rose, let me feel you. Just let me make you feel good. I don't need anything else."

She stopped and looked at him. "You don't want anything else? Jesus, Jack. I don't want you to pity me." She tried to wriggle away and he took her chin in his hand.

"Look at me." His voice was harsh and commanding. She did and he ground himself into her, the ridge of his cock getting right into that spot he wanted so badly. "You think I wouldn't kill to be inside you right now? " She gasped as he rolled his hips. "But that's not going to happen. You just got a bomb dropped on your house, and I was flying the fucking plane. I'm not taking advantage of you. It would be like taking you while you were drunk. But I'm a selfish bastard, so I'm going to get something. I'm going to get the feel of you and the smell and the taste if you'll let me. I'm going to take the memory of pleasuring you to my grave."

He arched up and drove in harder and faster. "Fuck! You are so beautiful." He kissed her as she panted, her cheeks pink and her mouth like ripe fruit. Her kisses were sinfully sweet. "Answer me, Rose. Are you going to give me just a little, even though I don't deserve it? Because if you aren't, then you need to go back upstairs. I can't be in this bed with you and not touch you." He rolled his hips, and she shuddered as she said his name. That's all he needed to hear as he slipped her t-shirt over her head. He put his hand under her back and lifted her pink nipple to his mouth. Her breasts were high and firm and so delicately pale, he almost released in his pants at the taste of her skin.

Rose felt his tongue to her toes. She'd never imagined this was what she was missing. He worshipped her, licking and sucking until the place between her legs throbbed. That's when he slid his hand between them and into her shorts. "Oh God, you feel perfect." He settled her on the pillow. "Let me see your eyes, love." Then he started. He pinned her to him with his blue eyes, hungry for her and filled with passion and longing. His fingers were expert. She'd done this to herself, of course, but it was never like this. He watched her face, figuring out just what she liked as she started to climb. He rubbed the top of her sex and the blood pounded in her ears. "That's it, sweet Rose. Let go. Come to me." Just as she threw her head back, he slid his finger deep. She contracted around it, climaxing in waves. She lost all sense of reality as he stayed with her, helping her ride it out. When she finally settled, she opened her eyes. The adoration on his face was palpable. He kissed her then, and she thought he'd cave in and come to her, but he didn't. He moved back down and kissed her breasts. They were live wires of sensation. Then he moved down her stomach. She started to panic. "Jack," her legs tensed.

"Rose, let me do this. I need your taste. I'll beg if you want." He nipped the spot below her navel. Then he cocked his head, "Has anyone ever pleasured you like this? Rose, don't look away. Answer me."

"No."

He swore with feeling. There a primal, pounding need in his body to have this from her and to give it. "Then we are definitely doing this. You'll like it, Rose. Just trust me. Let me take you higher." Her legs loosened and his eyes never left hers as he slid her shorts off. At the first touch of his tongue she almost came apart again, but she wanted to savor this. She'd always wondered. She watched him swallow. "Not yet. I'm planning on taking my time with this. Hold back until you can't stand it anymore. Just don't look away. I love watching you." He licked her more deeply now. He shook his head. "So sweet. It's almost too much to bear." He drank her in, moaning as he consumed her. She ran her hands in his thick, beautiful hair. "Jack," she moaned. He used just the tip of his tongue to tease, driving her wild. Then he spread her thighs with his two big hands and got serious, until she was out of her mind. He reached up just as she started to come and palmed both her breasts, his wide shoulders pinning her hips. He lightly pinched her nipples and it felt like her whole body was firing off. She arched, wanting more, wanting all of it. She rolled her hips and watched her own body give way. Watched as he took her orgasm deeply into himself, the triumph in his eyes as she released. It went on and on, a series of hills and valleys that seemed to have no end.

Rose woke with the light coming in the window. She was still nude. She'd tried to help Jack. He was painfully hard, but he wouldn't let her. She knew why. He was already punishing himself for getting involved with her. He was risking a lot to protect her, and he wouldn't make love to her because that would be the final blow to his sense of honor. She heard him in the shower and she wanted to see him. Even if he wouldn't let her touch him, he'd seen every inch of her, and what was good for the goose...and all that.

She opened the door to the steaming bathroom. The shower was huge and glass and blessedly transparent. He had one of those luxury showers with five hundred jets coming from all angles. But the shower appraisal stopped as she saw what he was doing. Jesus, that thick arousal of his was almost to his navel. What would that feel like inside her? He was leaning on one arm, stroking himself with the other. She let out a soft sigh, and his eyes shot to hers. Instead of being embarrassed, he put his head back and moaned, stroking harder as he took in her nude form. It was an in-your-face show of masculinity. Nary a blush or a stutter as he worked himself while she watched. She leaned into the doorway, not daring to look away. As he met her eyes again, he stroked his cock with purpose. She wished the water droplets and steam weren't impeding the show, because he was so gloriously naked and wet and was so beautiful as she watched him start to go over the edge. He shouted as he came, milking his release. He took a minute to catch his breath. Then he pulled her into the shower and punished her for watching him by dropping to his knees.

HE'D BEEN on the video conference in his office for about fifteen minutes. She didn't eavesdrop, but the tones were heated. When he came in, his jaw was tight. "What is it, Jack?"

"Nothing that you need to worry about, love." His face softened and he moved in close. "Give me your mouth, Rose."

She arched her neck, and he kissed her with thorough attention and skill. She felt it to her toes. He pulled away, the kiss improving his mood. "I'll take you to your father. They're moving him to a public holding facility. They don't want you knowing where they keep prisoners. We go in an hour."

"Jack, after this, I need to go to work. I'm supposed to be in at three."

"Rose, we talked about this."

"Yes, we did. You just didn't listen. I'm not compromising

this mission by making Luce suspicious. Maybe I can help." His faced darkened. "Why can't I help? You want to avenge your brother. Luce has a soft spot for me. Surely you've noticed."

"Yes, I have. And Hammer watches you like a vulture. Has it ever occurred to you that it's because you look like your mother?"

She furrowed her brow. "What are you saying, Jack? Do you think they already know who I am?"

"I don't think Hammer would stay quiet if he did. I do wonder, sometimes, about Luce. He's Irish, Rose. Do you know how your parents met? Do you know how your father and mother ended up mixed up with the Fallen?"

"No, I mean, maybe my gran knows, but she's not one to share."

"I think your father owes you the truth. It could help piece together what happened to your mother. When I watch Luce look at you, there's something in his eyes. An old hurt, maybe. Is it possible he was in love with your mother?"

Rose shook herself. "I don't know. I'm just starting to remember her again. I don't think that's something a child would've picked up on.

"But a man who loved his wife would pick up on it. Men don't respond well to other men sniffing around their women. I'm sure my colleagues have already tried to plant a seed of doubt about who actually murdered your mother, and it's a legitimate suspicion. The man who offered the intel is in prison still. I don't know if he's here in London, or somewhere else. Sometimes they move gang members away from their support system. Isolate them. I'll look into it because I want to interview him. What you have to decide, Rose, is how far you are willing to go to get the truth out of your father. He may end up complicit in some of their activity."

"My father was no father. He hid us in Ireland, yes. But he sent my grandmother just enough money to get by. He doesn't even know his own son. He's a criminal, and he might be covering for murderers, drug dealers, and human traffickers. The only thing I want from him is an HLA sample and some answers about my mother. Then he can go to the devil."

CHAPTER 8

*N*igel paced behind his desk. "Christ, Jackson. What the hell were you thinking taking her to one of your properties? You have completely lost your objectivity! I have a mind to yank you from this case right now!"

"But you won't because if Rose and I both disappear, you will lose any shot at Luce. You'll have to let her father go because you don't have shit on him. I've read the interview notes. He hasn't given you anything. You need Rose to get to him."

Nigel's forehead was sweating, and the vein along the side of his neck was pronounced. He had polished manners, as his job demanded. Being a director took a modicum of finesse. Right now, Jack saw the brutish side that he'd heard about when Nigel was a younger, lower-ranking agent. Had the nickname Boots. "You think you're the first one to get a cockstand for a pretty mark?" He gave a disgusted grunt. "I thought you were immune to this sort of thing, but apparently you're human under all that polish. So, if you need to fuck her to get it out of your system, by all means, slam one home old boy. Then get what information you can from her and ship the little tart back to Belfast."

Jack bristled. "She's no tart, and you need to back off Nigel. I'm not talking about this with you. If you want to fire me, good luck closing this case."

"Everyone is expendable, Jackson. Everyone. Now let's get the two of them in the same room and see if she can get him to talk."

* * *

Rose stood in the doorway of the room with no windows. When she'd appeared, her father paled, like he'd seen a ghost. Any doubt about her looking like her mother was gone. All but the eyes. When she looked at her father, older now, a small bit of gray at his temples, all she really took in was his eyes. The same ones she looked at every day in the mirror. The darkest brown, sad, ancient. He took a ragged breath as his eyes closed. Like he couldn't bear to look at her. He was as handsome as she remembered. Thick, shapely brows, tan skin, muscled arms. His hair was longer now. Just past his shoulders. Midnight hair but for the strands of silver. Dark Irish, her grandmother would say. He was English, yes, but he was half Irish by blood. She'd seen pictures of his parents. The father had been fair-haired and had gray eyes. A steel-worker by trade. His mother had been a raven-haired beauty with dark eyes and the look of the selkies from Irish lore.

"Hello, Da." She cursed her traitorous heart as her eyes began to well with tears. His face was pained as he saw her emotion. She shook herself. No. She would not give him absolution. He'd likely gotten her mother killed with his dodgy lifestyle. She clenched her jaw, walked to the table, and sat. "Have you gotten the test results back yet?"

He just shook his head. She slapped the table, and he

didn't even flinch. He was so hard. "Say something for feck sake!"

"No, Rosie. The tests are not back. If it comes up a match, feel free to drain me dry. Now, why the hell didn't you tell me sooner that he was sick?"

She pointed a finger at him. "How dare you get pissy with me! You haven't seen him since he was in nappies and ripped from his mother's breast! How could you just leave us? Why didn't you stay in Ireland and get away from..." She threw her hand up. "You know what? It doesn't matter. You made your choice. You gave your children away, didn't look back, and stayed with the bastards that probably killed her!"

"Those bastards helped me avenge her. Christ, you have got a mouth on you for a good Catholic. Do you talk to your patients like that, Rosie?"

"Stop calling me that! That's not my name anymore. Or Rosebud or any other pet name you had for me. You severed yourself off like an amputation!" Then she paused. "How did you know I was a nurse?"

He smiled sadly. "Did ye really think I didn't check on you? You're an emergency services nurse. You just finished school. Your brother is in his second year..."

She cut him off. "Why did you stay away?" When he said nothing, she leaned in. "Why, Da?"

"It was the one thing your granny demanded. I agreed because it was safer for you. I gave her my word that I wouldn't come to see you. She blamed me for Annalise."

"With bloody good reason! Why would you take her into that environment? Why couldn't you just get a job and be a decent husband and father?"

"I was a good husband! And I didn't take her to that environment, she took," he stopped, clenching his jaw, then looking at the two-way mirror. "It doesn't matter. You need to go home. Today, Rosie. Before you get too deep into my world. It's no place for you."

"Why in the hell did you stay? Why did Gran lie to me and tell me she drowned? How could you stay there after that?" Rose was crying now. "I lost her. Not just literally. My memory was completely erased. I had nothing but pictures of her. It's come to my understanding recently that it's possible I saw something. That I witnessed her murder. You need to tell me more about that weekend. I need to remember."

Jack watched this heartbreaking reunion and wanted to run in that room and beat the truth out of Mick Tierney. Then he watched the transformation come over his face. He really didn't know who'd killed his wife, and he didn't know that Rose may have witnessed it. He looked like he was going to pass out.

Rose said, "Where was she when she disappeared? Why wasn't she with you? Why weren't we all with you?"

Mick cleared his throat. "You stayed away because my sister's child had the measles. You'd been vaccinated, but Kieran hadn't been. I went alone because my sister's older child was having her first communion. Your mum told me to go ahead, that she'd stay back with you." He swallowed hard. Rose took in the tattoos and jail scrubs. His appearance was at odds with his words. "I loved my family. I was young when we married and had children, but I was a good father and an even better husband. I lived for Annalise. We were joined at the hip, usually. And the one time I left her." He choked on a sob. "The one time I took my eyes off her, she was taken. She had a six year old and a five month old, and someone took her from us and killed her. It was a gang war that had nothing to do with either of us!"

"You were in one of those feckin' gangs!"

"I was, but only because we liked the bikes and Luce was an old friend of your mother's. I held off becoming a prospect for years. I never fully joined. She and I stayed on the fringes and I worked as a mechanic. I worked for the club members and supported us with that money."

Rose didn't understand. "I remember patches on your jacket! You're a liar!"

He shook his head. "I had patches on my vest. Everyone did. But I never had a club patch. Not until after…"

"After my mother died." It wasn't a question. "Why?"

"It was a rival gang. We went on rides with the M.C., went to their parties now and again. I don't know why. Maybe to get at Luce. He didn't have a wife, but Annalise was an old friend. She'd been friends with his sister back in Ireland."

"So mam introduced you? Why did you stay after she died?"

"No man that calls himself a man would let his wife's murder go unavenged. We figured it out easy enough. A few of the men had connections throughout the biker community." He looked at his hands. "And these were no longer clean enough to raise two children."

That's when Jack watched Nigel walk in. Oh shit. He hadn't sprung it on him yet. "That's where your first mistake happened, Mr. Tierney. You were barking up the wrong tree. You started a war with the Outlaws over your wife's death, and it's looking more and more like Annalise was killed by a Sons of the Fallen member."

"That's a load of bollocks! They all loved Annalise. Luce loved her like a sister!"

"Like a sister, eh? Are you sure about that? Miss Tierney, do you want to weigh in on this? I mean, you've seen that longing in Luce's eyes when he looks at you." He looked back at Mick, "Looks like her mother, does she?"

Mick jumped off the table and the cuffs bit into his arms. "No! It wasn't like that!"

"Maybe not. Maybe it wasn't a love triangle. Maybe one

of those other barbarians took liberties while you were off with your sister instead of protecting your family. Maybe they didn't like having their advances spurned?"

Rose felt a rush come to her head. Her mother's voice. *Keep your hands off me! Get out of my house!* Then it was gone. She opened her eyes and shook her head.

Jack came over the speaker. "That's it! She's done."

Nigel cursed. "Christ, man. At least pretend you have a job," he said dryly.

He gently took Rose's arm. "Time is up. I'll call the lab and check on those results. You can call your brother at the hospital and check on him."

Mick's eyes flared and he sat up ramrod straight. "What is wrong with him? Is there something else going on with him?" His voice was panicked. "You don't have shit on me. You are holding me illegally. You need to let me out of here!"

"So you can warn your brothers? I think not." Nigel's voice was calm and smooth, and so condescending, even Jack felt like punching him.

"Rose, don't leave. I need more time, goddammit! You can't go back to that club!"

She turned on him and pointed. "If you don't have the sense or the balls to find out what really happened, then it's up to me!"

They closed the door to his screams.

Jack watched Nigel lead her through the door and expected Rose to be in tears. As soon as she got clear of the locking door, she wheeled on Nigel and slapped him right across the face. "You smug English bastard." Then she looked at Jack, stalked over, and slapped him too. He can't say he didn't have it coming, and it had been worth it to see Nigel get his ticket punched. She stomped down the hall, and he looked at Nigel. The man was rubbing his jaw and smiling. "Now I see the appeal. I always did like Irish women."

* * *

AFTER MAKING SOME CALLS, Rose sat in Nigel's office utterly defeated. That's when the tears came. "I'm sorry, Miss Tierney. Despite this bloody business, I was hoping for the best." Her father wasn't a match.

Jack took her by the arm and led her out of his boss's office. "You'll keep trying. We've already reached out to the sister."

"Thank you," she croaked. "Why can't my family catch a break?"

Nigel came down the hall after them. "Nigel, not now. Give her a minute."

"Sorry, I can't. This is important. I spoke with Dr. Lovington. She's a clinical psychologist with our organization. She specializes in forensic psychology. She helps us with victims, witnesses, and criminal profiling. I think it would be good for Miss Tierney to speak with her."

"I've tried shrinks. No one helped. I even tried hypnosis."

"She's good at what she does. She's at the top of her field. It won't hurt and it can only help. You remembered something in that room. I saw it." Jack had seen it too.

"It was just a quick flash. Just a voice. Nothing concrete." She said, but she was looking at Nigel. "You think she can give me a push. Is that it?"

"Think of it as helping you open a door. She's on her way. Let me order some lunch for you. You need to eat and take a break before we start this again. It isn't going to be a garden party."

She snorted. "Christ, could you be any more English? Are you going to set a full tea service?" Nigel smiled at that, and it occurred to Jack that he respected Rose. Earning his respect wasn't easy, and Jack felt a surge of pride.

"Nothing so grand, I'm afraid. We have a kebab stand a

block over, or fish and chips. The cuisine of choice for smug English bastards."

* * *

ROSE SAT across from a fiftyish woman. She was slim and well-aged with smart eyes. She was polished. Not the typical, underpaid, community counselor. "Agent De Clare tells me that you've been hypnotized before. Let's talk about that. Were there any devices used?"

"No. I was just supposed to picture my calm place. I was very relaxed, but I'm not sure I went under or anything of the sort. It seemed like a load of shite to be honest." The woman smiled, not commenting.

"It's also in your file that you're a musician."

"Yes. Piano and fiddle."

"That's good. Then you're familiar with a metronome. It's not magic. It's just a way for you to focus both with your eyes and ears. It helps you enter the relaxed trance-like state that will leave you open to suggestion. Then I'll try to take you backward to find those suppressed memories. It may not work right away. You may remember what are to be considered irrelevant incidents, but the door will be open and memories could gradually come back to you. I have to warn you, despite my colleague's investigation, this could be traumatizing for you if you recall something violent. I'm here to do the hypnosis, but I'd be remiss if I didn't tell you to follow up with a therapist. My purpose here is evidence collection for the agency, but I don't want to downplay how this is going to affect you. "

Rose nodded. "And if I don't remember anything traumatic or criminal, will I still get the memories of my mam back?"

"Yes. It's possible that your mother's death was enough

trauma, even if you didn't know the circumstances. With a closed casket, your lack of closure could have been enough to tax your mind."

"But you don't think so."

"I don't know you, Miss Tierney. I can't speculate."

"But you don't think so," Rose repeated, lifting her chin and meeting the woman's eyes.

"No. I don't. I think you saw something with enough emotional trauma that ripped a chasm in your memories. Our personalities develop, but some traits are noticeable early in childhood. I'd wager that you were strong-minded as a young girl?" Rose's mouth lifted on one side, conceding the point. "It takes a fair bit of stress to the brain to cause this sort of repression. You didn't lose your mother. You hid her. You put her somewhere because the thought of her in any way scared the hell out of you. You may even be dealing with severe survivor guilt for not being able to stop whatever you saw. If you'd had a head injury or oxygen deprivation, something physical to explain it, I'd wonder. If your mother had been abusive, I'd understand some black-outs as well. This seems to specifically surround her death, and you suffered no physical injury. Your mind is protecting you. Yes, Miss Tierney, I think you saw something. I'd stake my career on it."

ROSE FELT herself drifting with the steady beat of the metronome. Her eyes becoming mesmerized by the back and forth motion. She could hear the doctor's voice. She asked her about her home as a child, having her picture and then describe her kitchen, her living room, her own bedroom with its pink drapery and wooden dollhouse. Then she moved to people. Her first teacher, her father, what her little brother looked like as a newborn baby. She eventually guided her calmly and gently into her mother's arms. Rose saw glimpses of her. Heard her voice. Heard her singing to her as she rocked Rose on one knee, Kieran cradled on the other side. She saw her parents dancing in the kitchen. U2 playing slowly in the background as her young parents kissed so sweetly. She ran, grasping their legs and looking up to them.

After a while, she heard the doctor's voice again. She went to the front door and tried to leave that happy home. Tried to walk to where the doctor was leading her. But the door was locked and she didn't have a key. She looked behind her and her father was in the kitchen. Her mother was gone. He was sitting at the table, sobbing as he held Kieran, trying to give him a bottle.

"Da, it's okay. Mam will feed him. He doesn't like the bottle. He likes how Mammy feeds him." Her father's sobs grew harder. *"Don't cry, Da. It's okay. Just call Mammy."*

"Rose, on the count of five you are going to wake. One, two, three, four, five."

When Rose came awake, her chest was heaving. Her face was soaked as she wept with great wracking sobs until she crumbled into herself on the cushioned chair. It was like she was trying to hold that little girl who had lost so much. She didn't even hear Jack come in, but then he was holding her. After she cried herself dry, she finally settled. She looked around the room, then looked at the doctor. "I didn't remember what we needed."

"I'm not surprised. I must warn you, this is just the beginning. You will start to have memories return to you. I woke you because your stress level was getting too high. That door was locked, and you were getting into some very heavy emotion. I want you to keep a diary. Everything you feel, hear, or see in your mind. Do you understand? Something that you think may be insignificant could actually be a piece to this puzzle." Rose nodded, wiping her nose on a tissue. "I'm sorry for your loss, Miss Tierney. How do you feel?"

Rose said, "Tired and sad. But I feel a little relieved as well."

"Relief about what specifically?"

"About remembering her and him, actually. Remembering them together. I guess I needed to know that it destroyed him as much as it did me. I don't want to hate him."

Jack gave her a squeeze. She looked at him. "Did you watch?"

"No, it was recorded. You don't have to tell me if it was too private, but I'm here for you if you want to talk ."

She swallowed hard, wiping another tear away. "I think I do."

* * *

JACK TOOK Rose back to the townhouse and heated up a bowl of soup for her and his sister. Her story came out slowly. When she got to the part about her father trying to give the baby a bottle, a child who'd been nursing and crying for his mother, it had broken Jack's heart. He actually pitied Mick Tierney, and Amelia had been horrified. They'd left out the part about Jack's job, and the fact that the psychologist worked for MI5. His sister didn't need to know that.

Apparently, the memory loss happened in degrees. Nigel had finally calmed Mick down and started asking specific questions about Rose's emotional withdrawal. According to Mick, she remembered nothing from her mother's disappearance. The father had come home to find a neighbor watching the kids. Rose had gone over when Kieran wouldn't stop crying. Rose couldn't tell them where the mother had gone. Mick knew that Annalise would have never left the children alone, so he'd called the police. The club wives had pitched in to watch the kids while they rode the streets looking for any sign of his wife. Her body washed up the next day.

Rose's complete memory loss happened later. Mick sat Rose down and told her that her mother was dead. Then he told her that they were going to go see her mother at the funeral home and then visit her granny in Ireland. Rose had shut down. She'd stared off into space and completely withdrawn from the world during the burial. She hadn't even cried. Not until he left her in Ireland. She'd screamed for him as he left the driveway. Begged him not to leave them.

When Amelia left to take a shower, they were alone. Jack told Rose everything Nigel had learned because she had a right to know.

She was quiet for a while, wiping silent tears. Then she straightened, steeling herself for the night to come. "I need to go to work, Jack. I need to get back to that club and see if anything comes back to me." Jack tensed. "I have to go. I owe it to my mother. I hid these memories and locked her away. I owe it to her."

"I understand. I have to switch cars with my friend and give Amelia mine. I'll take the bike and be there about an hour after your shift starts."

"What if I never remember?" She couldn't bear the thought.

"Then maybe it's a blessing. This is taking a toll on you, Rose. I hate it." he said softly. Then he pulled her to his mouth, and his kiss was like an apology and a promise all in one. "I won't let anything happen to you."

CHAPTER 9

ose took a pint of lager into Luce's office. He'd been having meetings all day, which was odd. He was meeting with some men from another chapter in South Wales and one closer to Cornwall. It was strange to think of these old coastal cities having gang activity, but she'd been serving men all day that were held over from Luce's celebration. Pembroke, Bristol, Truro, and Cardiff all represented. One of the Cornwall men had bragged, "Once a smuggler, always a smuggler. Can't go failin' the bloodline now, can I?" She wondered about that as she watched stern, leather-clad men do some sort of business with Luce. Drugs, perhaps? After what had happened to Jack's brother, it was very possible.

She put the pint down on his desk, and he took her arm, stopping her retreat. "You seem off today, dear Rose."

"I'm a bit tired. I had a fitful night."

"Thank you for the music. It was like being home again." His face was as gentle as she'd ever seen it. Had he really been in love with her mother?

114

"You don't talk much about home. Do you miss your family?" She cocked her head in question.

"This is my family. The only family I had who was worth a damn is in her grave twenty-seven years."

"Your mother?"

"No, lass. My mother was a drunk. The best thing she ever did was leave. My father didn't do us the courtesy. I'm talking about my sister."

Rose wondered if this was the sister that had brought her mother into his life. "I'm sorry for it Luce. Losing a sibling is its own unique pain. I can't imagine it." She squeezed his shoulder. She hoped like hell that despite his life of hardness and crime, he hadn't been the one to kill her mother. She didn't feel anything ominous when she was near him. She had a flash of memory just as she turned to walk away from him. She was running through the club. Everything was in the same place, but a little newer. *Uncle Luce!* And she ran into his arms. His face was unclear, but his beard was darker. *How's my little Irish Rose?*

"Rose? Are you sure you're feelin' well?"

Rose looked up into his eyes. "Yes, Luce. I'll do. I need to get back to the bar." She walked in just as Jack came through the door. A few people shouted, "Jackknife!" He spoke to Sammy and another one of the M.C. brothers that had brought his kids to the party yesterday. His wife left early with them before the heavy partying started. Rose wondered how some of these men could be involved with the criminal element of Luce's dynasty. Then again, her father had a family and he was hip deep in this world. He'd married when he was closer to Kieran's age. He'd resisted becoming a prospect until her mother died. Had he pulled the trigger on the rival gang deaths? Had that act been what had caused him to break fully from civil society?

Jack sat across from Rose, nodding when she offered to

get him a beer. She thought about what he'd done to her last night and then again in his shower. The feel of his mouth on her sex. The utter bliss of reaching her climax while with a man. As if he was reading her mind, his eyes grew hooded. "There's leftover birthday cake by the juke box," she said lightly.

"Nothing could be as sweet as what I had last night," he purred. He smiled as her face blushed. She wiped the bar down nervously.

"Aye, well. It was rather delicious for me as well." She felt bold as she said the words. Then she noticed Jack's brows turned down. "Is something wrong?"

He leaned in. "That's the third time my work phone has vibrated in my pocket. I need to go somewhere private." He slid the beer back. "Keep that cold and I'll be back. I need to go down the block." She put the beer in the cooler, wondering what was going on. Luce forbid cell phones, but Jack kept his on silent and had it anyway, along with a small pistol hidden in his waistband. He walked out and passed Hammer walking in. Luce's voice came from behind her, "Hammer! We need to talk, brother! Rose, bring him a pint!" Just as she started to pour the beer, Candice walked by Hammer and he grabbed her by the waist, pulling her tight up against him. That's when she heard it again. Her vision dimmed and she heard her mother say, *Keep your hands off me! Get out of my house!* Then the male voice, *That young buck of yours isn't here, is he?*

Rose dropped the pint glass as it shattered against the floor, beer splashing everywhere.

"Rose, are ye okay?" Luce narrowed his eyes and looked between her and Hammer. "Is something going on that I need to know about?"

Hammer shrugged, "I've got no idea, brother. Just looking

for a bit of fun. Let's get this meeting over with, so I can get some quality time.

Luce ignored him. "What is it, lass? You look like you've seen a ghost."

A voice behind him spoke. "I suppose she has. Haven't you Rosie?"

They all turned, and Rose's stomach dropped as she saw him. "Hello, Da."

* * *

JACK CALLED and Katherine picked up on a oner. "He's out, Jack. Some civil liberties lawyer came banging on the door, and we had to release him. It just happened a half hour ago. Where are you? Why didn't you pick up?"

"I was on the bike, then in the club. Jesus, Katherine. I need to get back in there!" Katherine shouted as he ended the call.

* * *

YOU COULD HAVE HEARD a pin drop in the club as everyone looked toward Mick Tierney. Luce yelled, "Everyone out. The club is closed for the night!" His order invited no protest. Everyone got up like the place was on fire and piled out the front entrance. Everyone but Hammer, who locked the front door. Rose assumed, given their greeting, that she was to stay as well. Luce looked her over, like he was trying to see into her very soul. "Can someone tell me what the fuck is going on here?"

Jack eased in the back, not wanting to show himself just yet. The fact that Luce made everyone leave and locked the door meant he couldn't just blend in with the other bar flies.

Luce met Rose's eyes. "I suspected, but I wasn't sure. You

don't have her eyes." He looked over at Mick and frowned. "Where have you been?"

Hammer sneered, "Yes, Mick. Tell us where you've been?"

"I'm assuming you already know since you called a civil rights lawyer."

Luce shook his head, his gaze narrowing on Hammer. "Talk or so help me God I will throttle you."

"Well, it seems Hammer's been keeping secrets again. I got picked up. I've been cooling in some federal holding facility having coppers crawl up my ass. Two weeks with no windows and no phone calls. Two fucking weeks and it didn't occur to anyone that maybe I'd been killed or arrested?"

Luce ground his jaw. "Jesus Christ, Mick. You had me out of my feckin' mind. Of course we looked for you. I accessed every back channel I have, and we checked every hospital within a hundred kilometers. I even sent one of the girls to the police station pretending to be your girlfriend." He took long strides over to Mick and pulled him into a tight hug. "Jaysus, Mick. You look like shit." He accent was thick with emotion.

Hammer's voice dripped venom. "That's it? Are you fucking with me? He's been in custody for two weeks and you hug him? Check the bastard for wires."

Luce turned on Hammer, "I've had enough out of you. Mick would never talk. Why didn't you tell me you'd found him?"

He paused for a moment, then said with a shrug, "I wasn't sure. It was a hunch. I told you I thought maybe he got grabbed on his trip to Belfast."

Rose had been so quiet, they'd almost forgotten about her. She snapped, "You were coming to Belfast? How often have you been there, Da? You do remember you have children nearby, right?"

"I heard about Kieran. I was going to come, Rosie."

"Stop calling me Rosie!" Rose realized immediately that her father had no intention of telling them that she had been brought in by MI5 as well. Hammer was lying to save face. She'd been the one to call the civil rights lawyer, not him. An anonymous tip. The more she'd learned about her father, the more she realized that he played no part in the drug smuggling or gun sales of the club. As Jack had put it, Mick was the cleanest of the bunch. One minor arrest for disturbing the peace from a biker rally where everyone had been ticketed. He may have turned a blind eye, but he was no drug dealer.

Had suspicion about her mother's death taken root? Or maybe he just didn't want them to hurt her. He cleared his throat. "You can check me all the way to the crack of my ass if you want. I'm not wearing a fucking wire. And I'm no bloody snitch, so watch your tongue, Hammer."

Hammer gave a derisive snort and Rose had that feeling again. Familiar. She couldn't put a finger on it. A chill went through her. "So that's why you came. You were looking for your father?" Luce asked. "Jesus, Rose. Why didn't you just ask me? Why would you leave home and sneak into my club? You've been here for almost two weeks."

"I didn't know if the two of you were on good terms! I was walking into the feckin' lion's den, Luce. Then I realized he was missing and I didn't know if someone did something to him. And given where he's been for the last two weeks, can you blame me?"

Mick said, "Well, you've found me. The rest is private between you and me." Her father turned to Luce. "They don't have shit on you, Luce. And they didn't get anything from me. Now, if you'll give me a few minutes, I need to speak with my daughter."

119

ROSE WALKED out the front door, and Jack was sitting strad-dled over his bike. "A friend of yours?" Her father eyed him suspiciously.

"That's none of your business." She took her phone out of her saddle bag.

"What are you doing?"

"Checking my messages. Kieran is still in the hospital." She lowered her brows. "Three missed calls from Gran. That's a bad sign."

Jack watched Rose make a quick phone call. Then she was mounting her bike. Her father grabbed her arm. "Wait, Rose! Tell me what the hell is going on!"

"He's sick, Da. And he needs me. You don't have what he needs, so you needn't bother getting any further involved."

"I'm going with you."

"The hell you are! I won't have you upsetting him or Gran. He doesn't even know you, Da. You left him before his first birthday." She motioned to the bar entrance. "For THAT. For them! You made your choice."

"I was trying to protect you!"

"Well, you succeeded. Now consider yourself relieved from duty. I'm going to protect us from now on. From you." She started her bike and Jack did the same. She left her father standing in the parking lot, and Jack followed behind her.

* * *

AMELIA WATCHED the flurry of activity as Rose packed her bag. "I booked the ferry for half seven. I need to get to Liverpool."

"Rose, I would have flown you home. Would you just stop and think for a minute?" Jack said.

"I don't need your help or your money. I have everything handled! Where the hell are my clear goggles?" She was stressed and spitting mad at her father.

Before Jack could argue, Amelia said from behind her laptop. "Done. Three economy tickets to Belfast. We need to leave for the airport in two hours and thirty minutes."

"Amelia." Rose's voice was more tender with her.

"Well done, love, but you need to cancel yours. You have class," Jack said.

"It's a bank holiday. I'm off until Tuesday," Amelia said with a grin. "I've never been to Belfast. I'm going. Rose needs support."

Rose screeched at him as he ran up the stairs. "I didn't invite you! Gran doesn't even have a pull-out!"

Rose came upstairs to find him rifling through an old chest. He sighed. "I'm going to need to go to my flat. The few clothes I have here won't do." He walked over to the door and closed it. "I found out where they are holding the man who tried to cut a deal by testifying about the two murders twenty years ago. One was your mother, the other a prospect with the M.C.. In the interview notes, he said that the Outlaws didn't kill your mother. That it was an inside job. Later he tried again, saying that the prospect that was killed during the gang conflict was also killed by an insider and it was just made to look like a rival gang hit. He was transferred to Maghaberry in Northern Ireland to cut him off from his gang affiliations."

"Are you going to interview him?" Rose asked, suddenly not angry with him.

"Yes, and this time I'll take him seriously. Someone should have followed up the first time he talked."

"The truth is, Jack, that no one gave a shit about some biker's old lady and a thug prospect." Rose knew she sounded bitter, but she couldn't help it.

"Two Outlaws died during that conflict. They probably assumed that it was a revenge killing and that her killers were dead." He took out his cell and dialed Katherine. After filling her in, he said, "We'll have a rental car waiting at the airport. I'll take you to the hospital before we do anything else. Now, tell me exactly why your granny called."

"They said he can't get out of bed without passing out. Anemia, maybe. He's weakened significantly in the last twenty-four hours. I need to get to him."

"And flying is the quickest way. I'll send a car for Amelia. Come with me to the flat. I'd like the company." His face was a bit vulnerable, and Rose wondered where he thought this was headed. Surely he understood that this relationship was doomed from the start.

Like an eejit, she said, "Give me two minutes."

ROSE LEANED back into the leather seats of the Jaguar and sighed. "This feels sinful." Jack watched her out of the corner of his eye as he shifted gears.

"I wish you were wearing a skirt," he said softly.

"Why?"

Then he ran his hand from her knee to the V of her thighs. She moaned. He pressed his hand into her and her hips jerked. "You are the devil."

"I like giving you pleasure, Rose. You can't imagine how much I get out of it."

"Aye, well. I'm quite mad for it myself." She said, almost miffed.

He gave her a devilish grin. They arrived at the flat and as she walked through the front door, he pulled her back and pressed her against the door. His mouth was firm and skillful as his hands explored her. He spoke against her mouth in between warm, thorough kisses. "I need to touch you again. You're so soft and warm, Rose. So wet." He started undoing the buttons on her jeans, then he brought her chin up to meet his eyes. He slid his hand into her pants. It only took a few skillful, slippery strokes and she was climaxing against his hand, her hips meeting his strokes. "I'm going to come, Jack. I can't hold…" A moan ripped from her throat and he kept at her until she could barely stand.

"That's it. That's what I wanted." He kissed her deeply, keeping his hand in place until her pulsing flesh had settled. She was like a drug. How the hell was he going to let her go?

CHAPTER 10

*R*ose walked into the hospital room just as her brother's nurse finished with his vitals. "Wendy dahling!"

She laughed, throwing her arms wide. "Peetah!" This was always their greeting after a long absence. A throwback from younger years when she read him the story of Peter Pan. She hugged him tightly, fighting the tears. She pulled back and rubbed the hair from his brow. "You look pale, Kieran. And you've lost more weight. Are you eating?"

"The food in here is shite. They should let me go home. I don't have pneumonia. My lungs are clear."

"And if they sent you home and you passed out? Granny would never be able to lift you, even with the weight you've lost." He'd been a big, strong young man. At nearly twenty, he had topped off at 6'2" and almost two hundred pounds. He was a looker, even diminished. A thick head of dark hair like their father and green eyes like their mother. He stiffened when he saw people in the doorway. "Kieran, I'd like you to meet my friend Jack and his sister Amelia. I met them in

London. Jack has some business here in Belfast so we flew together."

She watched Kieran's face take in the visitors. Jack looked different. He'd shaved and was wearing jeans and an athletic pullover that accentuated his impressive build. Kieran sat up in his bed, looking prickly. Then his eyes landed on Amelia. She was dressed for autumn with dark jeans, a smart looking tweed hat, and equestrian style boots, or boot in this case. Her other foot was in a soft cast and orthopedic boot. "You'll pardon my appearance. You aren't catching me at my best." His tone held a note of bitterness.

Amelia said lightly, "We've just traveled like cattle in economy class. I'm a bit out of sorts myself."

He narrowed his eyes at her. "London was it?" He looked at Rose, "I'd thought we'd had our fill of Englishman."

Jack ignored the jibe and put his hand out. "Jack De Clare. I've heard a lot about you, Kieran."

"Been telling my tale of woe, Rose? Well, don't throw a charity ball or anything. I'll be back in fighting shape before you know it. Or dead. Either way, don't waste your pity."

Amelia bristled. "The only one I pity right now is your sister."

"Why is that?" his brow raised.

"Because you're a grown man acting like a snide teenager, and you're probably embarrassing her. Don't worry, Rose. He's sick, so we'll ignore the fact that he's being a prat."

Rose clapped a hand over her mouth as she stifled a laugh. That's when they got the first genuine grin out of Kieran. "You've got some backbone under that designer jumper, English."

She folded her arms over her chest. "Yes, I do. So it's best you mind your manners."

That's when he noticed the boot. "What happened to you? Lose an ass-kicking contest?"

The side of her mouth turned up. "Quite the contrary. You should see the other guy."

Rose and Jack just watched the tennis match with amusement. Jack pulled Rose aside. "I'm going to go to the inn to change my clothes. I'm headed to the prison. It goes without saying, Amelia thinks I'm going to a boring business meeting." He popped his head back in the hospital room. "Amelia, love. I'm going to go get us checked in at the bed and breakfast. Are you ready?"

Amelia looked at Rose, then Kieran. "If it's okay, I think I'll stay. I don't have a car and I can call a lift if I get tired." They'd rented a car at the airport, but they were all three headed for different destinations. He hesitated.

"My gran will be here in a half hour. She'll take her where she needs to go. Go on, Jack. Do what you need to do. I'll see you in the morning."

Kieran leaned in and whispered to Amelia. "I think your brother's got it for my sister."

"Shh," she replied. "We're all in denial."

"I can hear you both," Jack said, shaking his head. Rose was flushed pink with embarrassment. "See you all in the morning."

* * *

JACK KNEW it was well past hours for visitors at the prison, but this was his opportunity to get some face time with William Miller before he had to go back to London. He couldn't be gone long from the club. He knew something was brewing, and with Mick out, it was crucial he be there. Mick had no idea who he was, thankfully.

The night guard said, "I could get in trouble with those civil rights types for waking him up for this."

It was only half past nine, so he doubted it, but he said,

"And I appreciate it greatly. I knew I could count on fellow law enforcement." An overweight prison guard was hardly law enforcement, but he needed this guy on his side. And working at a maximum security prison had to be a rough way to earn his pay.

"Just wait in here and he'll be escorted down in a few minutes."

As the man came in, Jack took in his appearance. He was surprised how old the man looked. His file put him at sixty, but he looked about ninety. Thin, a deeply lined face, and tattoos covering every inch including his neck. This guy was hard core. "Mr. Miller, I'm Agent Declar." He varied his name a bit, technically keeping it legal while mussing up the pronunciation. "I've been told you've waived any sort of counsel?"

"Fucking lawyers have never helped. I'm going to die in here unless you have some sort of deal in mind. I want to meet my grandson before I go to hell." He had a northern accent, maybe Manchester or York.

"That's going to depend on what you have to tell me. I've been told you have stage four lung cancer that has gone to your liver. If you can help me, I'll do my best to get you out before you meet your maker."

"Try isn't good enough. I want a deal. That bastard I killed to get in here was a piece of shit. He raped my old lady's daughter after her football practice. He was the bloody coach. I should have gotten a medal for that kill."

"You don't have a lot of time. Your treatments are expensive. I'd wager that the government would love to get you home and out of their hair. Let me be perfectly clear and advise you that if you don't talk to me, I'll make sure you die in here."

The man cursed. "I know that my brothers didn't kill that Tierney woman. I know it for sure."

"Go on. How do you know?"

"Because we were pulling a warehouse burglary in Manchester with another chapter that weekend. Both the men they took out were innocent. Well, at least of that crime. Our gang did not kill Mick Tierney's old lady. Whatever intel they got was bullshit. And we didn't take out that prospect either. He was a schoolmate of my son. He was a decent enough lad. Our president didn't want a war with Luce's boys. We were working on a deal with some guns they had coming in. He took credit for the prospect's murder so it looked like we'd had our payback. Then they called a cease fire."

"Who put together this deal? Luce?"

"No, it was his second. Luce lost his mind when that woman got killed. He's the one that rode with Mick to take out our two men. It was an ugly scene. Our numbers were dwindling and there was no way could we sustain an all-out war with the Fallen. So we rolled over and played dead for a while. Our president was sure things would get back to where they were, but they never did. Luce holds a grudge."

"I have notes on your other interviews. Why do you think it was an inside job?"

"That prospect that was killed from the Fallen? He came to the house. He was looking for my son, but the boy was living with his mother at the time. He'd been beaten. Said he couldn't go back to the club. He didn't want Luce asking questions." He rubbed his jaw, shaking his head. "My old lady cleaned him up, fed him, made him a bed on the couch. He had a couple of drinks and broke down. He said he'd done something he couldn't live with. That he was afraid of his own club. He was having second thoughts about joining. I pressed him for details, but he wouldn't come out with the full story. He just said that any men that would hurt a woman, he couldn't hang with. He just broke down like a child and cried. Mick's old lady washed up in the river the next day. I always thought the two were related. Seeing how I knew our men didn't do it, I started thinking maybe one of them did. They hit our guys two days later, and then Jimmy, the lad that had slept on my couch, shows up dead with his throat cut." He looked Jack in the eyes. "I swear on my grandson's life, our club didn't take that kid out. All I know is that he knew something or had done something that he couldn't live with, and he was thinking about bailing on his M.C.. You ask me? Whoever took out Tierney's old lady cut that lad's throat to keep him quiet. Then framed our club."

* * *

JACK CALLED Nigel after the interview. "Why are you waking me up, Jackson?" Jack smiled at his bristly tone.

"My, my. You do go to bed early. You obviously can't arrange for someone to keep you up late." He heard the bedding rustle as the jibe hit home. He liked making Nigel shed his manners.

"Piss off. Talk or I'm firing you." He told him about the interview, and about the promise he'd made to arrange compassionate release. "Yes, well I think I can arrange that. If his medical report is to be believed, the poor sod is a goner. It's a pity we don't have a more solid lead."

"Yes, but we have Rose. We had Mick, but you let the bastard out. Thanks for the heads up, by the way. Things got very tense with Rose in the room. She's your only potential witness and I walked into that powder keg unaware."

"Luce wasn't happy to see him, then?"

"Actually, Luce was overjoyed. Hammer was the one put out. He wanted him checked for wires."

"I still can't figure out how they knew we had him."

"Lucky guess after ruling out other theories, I'd imagine."

Jack laughed to himself. He'd bet his Jaguar title that Rose had called that attorney. He'd seen it in her eyes after the hypnosis, when she'd said, *I don't want to hate him.*

And who could blame her. He was the only parent she had left, despite the fact that he'd checked out twenty years ago.

As he ended the call, he checked his text messages. Amelia had not gone to the Bed and Breakfast that he'd arranged. She was at Rose's home. Jesus, what the hell was he doing? He'd mixed his private life with his business life and his sister was female-bonding with the O'Maolin household. Then he thought about Rose. Her sweet, pink cheeks that brightened when he kissed her. Her liquid brown eyes that told him more about her than anything else. Innocent. He thought about his sister's warning. To be careful with Rose, because she'd had a rough start with men. His neck prickled with anxiety, because if he found out she'd been hurt by a man, he might hunt the bastard down and beat him to death. The protective instincts that he felt with Rose were a bad sign. He was in over his head with her. He didn't want to break her heart. He laughed out loud. Who the hell was he kidding? For the first time in his life, he feared for his own heart.

He followed the GPS to the small street in Ballyclare. The house was tiny. Barely big enough for the three who lived in it. But the yard was tidy and the garden was strewn with roses, lavender, and herbs. It was an older, stern looking woman that met him as he approached the house. She had auburn hair that was streaked with silver, and she had sharp green eyes. She wasn't what he'd expected. The term granny brought to mind a soft, smiling woman with a white bun and an apron. She was an attractive woman and he saw where Rose got her looks. He imagined that if he put photos of the three generations next to each other, he'd see even more of a resemblance. His heart softened for the woman. She wore jeans and an oversized jumper, despite her slimness. She'd lost her daughter and inherited two kids in the bargain. "Good evening, Miss..." He stopped himself before he revealed too much. Rose had never told him her grandmother's last name.

"O'Maolin, but Keirsty will do." A dog ran from around her legs and greeted him before he'd even reached the door.

"Hello there." He was a border collie. Jack liked dogs. He'd never had one, but he liked them.

"And that is Laddie. He's friendly enough. Come in. The girls are in the kitchen cleaning up."

Jack followed the sound of music. Some remake of *Smooth Criminal.* He smiled broadly at the two women that had their backs to him. They were singing and dancing like utter fools. It was adorable. Rose was trying to do the moon walk with a sponge in her hand, while Amelia was pulling off one of the iconic Michael Jackson moves. "Michael Jackson did it better," he said over the music. Rose screeched and the sponge flew out of her hand.

Amelia did another slick move, keeping the weight off her air cast. "Not a chance, brother!" Rose turned the music off, obviously embarrassed.

He approached Amelia and tugged on her hair. "I meant the song of course, not the dancing. Aren't you supposed to be staying off that foot?"

"Oh, I have been. They've had me on the sofa for over an hour with an ice pack and a cuppa Granny's special tea."

"Well, I can't argue with Granny's tea."

Rose's grandmother eyed him suspiciously, then looked at her granddaughter. It occurred to him he was still in the suit. Amelia was accustomed to seeing him like this, but Rose wasn't. He was clean shaven and had his hair combed into a more manageable arrangement. He suddenly wanted his leather back. A foolish part of him thought that Rose wouldn't like him like this. She'd made comments about him being a viscount with a silver spoon in his mouth. There was no way he was going to tell her he was next in line for a Barony. If his father's older brother kicked it without an heir, he was it. Nope, no way was he telling her that. It would just confirm her fears that they were too far apart in social class.

It didn't matter one bit to him. He looked around the small home and felt a stirring in his chest. There were pictures of Rose and Kieran spread around. The furniture was old, but well kept. Lovely, country antiques giving it just the right touch. A beautiful, carved crucifix to the left of the front door. The kitchen was cozy. Lined with ceramic tile and white cabinetry. A small plaque of St. Martha was over the cooker. His eyes landed on Rose, then. She looked defensive and unsure. "You have a lovely home, Keirsty. It's warm and inviting. Your primitive antiques are quite something."

Keirsty turned up a half smile. "Aye, I'm an antique dealer. It doesn't pay much, but it supports the habit."

He smiled at that. "And who is St. Martha?"

"The patron saint of cooking and hospitality. Heavens, where are my manners. Sit, Mr. De Clare, and have a bit of tea. You must be knackered. It's nearly midnight."

"Please call me Jack. And a cup of tea would be just the thing. Thank you." He sat and Rose went by him to help. He grabbed her hand and she looked down at him. He squeezed it and tried to send her a message with his eyes. He didn't think less of her for this humble, loving home. He thought more of her. Suddenly all of his cold, empty properties with their exquisite furnishings just seemed lonely. "Will you give me a tour, Rose? I couldn't see very well, but the garden was beautiful. Was that your doing?"

She smiled, tears threatening. "We all pitch in. Well, Kieran does on his good days." Her throat worked convulsively as she fought the emotions.

"Then let's walk, and you can tell me what the doctor said."

He turned to Keirsty who watched them, her eyes somehow gentler. "Would you mind if I take that around with me. I'll be careful. My mother would box my ears for leaving the table with her Dresden." He said with a self-deprecating smile.

"Well, we're not so formal here. You can be easy, lad." She looked at his sister. "The both of you look like you could do with a bit of easy."

Amelia walked over to Keirsty and put an arm around her. "Will you adopt me? My grandmother smacked my knuckles during piano lessons and made me wear pinafores."

Keirsty said, "I'm an acquired taste, darlin'. The novelty might wear off and then ye won't be so mad for the idea. I assign chores and am an extremely nosey granny." She gave Rose a side glance and they all laughed as she handed a teacup to Jack. Then he followed Rose out of the kitchen.

JACK TOOK IN THE SMALL, neat bedrooms. Rose's had a small, oak, spoon-carved Victorian bed, a downy comforter of the palest blue. She had a large black and white photograph that had been printed on stretched canvas. She and her brother bracketed their granny as they posed by the dramatic rock formations of Giant's Causeway. Her hair was spiraling in a gust of sea air, her mouth open and laughing. She looked about twenty. Her brother a lanky adolescent who kissing his granny on the cheek.

She noticed his gaze. "A tourist took that. Some man from Beijing. I just liked it. It was a grand time for us. A day drive one Saturday when the weather was fair."

He rubbed his hand over her hair and she leaned into the

contact. "It was a hard day. First the showdown with your father, then the hospital. How are you holding up?" They walked out the back of the house, into the garden.

She smiled sadly. "I'll do. I've got no choice, have I? I have to be okay."

"You can lean on other people, though. I mean, I know you're some kind of bloody superhero but you are allowed to ask for support. I'd like to do that for you. Be that for you."

"I can't lean on people who aren't in it for the long road, Jack. This is a case to you. When you've gone as far as you can with this, you'll move on. Amelia will go back to school. This will be a single snapshot for you, but it's my life." She pointed to her chest as she said it. "You'll go to your posh house and your power suits and I'll be wearing scrubs and working the night shift at the hospital trying to make ends meet. This isn't your life, Jack. Playing nice with my granny and sipping tea in a little working class house probably seems fun, but that won't last. You don't see me. Not really. You see an idea of me, but we are too different."

"You're wrong, Rose! I do see you!" He cupped her elbows, willing her to look at him. "I watched you when you weren't paying me any mind. I saw you go face to face with Luce and Hammer and your father and anyone else who got in your way. I watched you with your brother, reading over his charts and taking charge of his care as soon as you walked through the door. You're smart and brave and loyal like no one I've ever met. I see you. And I don't give a damn what house you live in or who your parents are. Not in the way you think. I'm proud to know you, Rose. I want to help because I care for you. I know you've got no reason to trust me and maybe you're right. Maybe I'm just torturing myself and it's doomed to crash and burn. But right now all I can think about is crawling into that little antique bed with you and kissing you until you can't breathe."

As the protest left her lips, he had her behind the garden shed. She moaned against his mouth as he curled his fingers in her hair. "Christ, Rose. You've got no bloody idea what this is doing to me. You think I'm some cold English bastard who's made of stone, but you're wrong." He rubbed his lips back and forth over her jawline, so soft and warm, memorizing the feel of her and the taste. He felt the dampness and tasted the salt from her tears. "Oh, Rose. Please, love, don't cry." He kissed her eyes, then took her mouth again, until she was wild against him. "Come to me. In the morning. Please, Rose. I need you. I need to hold you. That scene in the pub with your father was murder. I nearly stormed in the room." He put his forehead to hers. "I don't like that you're involved in this. I hate it." This time she lifted her mouth, kissing the corners of his mouth. They heard the laughter coming from the kitchen window, Amelia giggling at something Granny had said. He said, "Come to me, Rose." His voice was low and hoarse.

Rose met his eyes and she was lost. Those stormy blue eyes that seemed to be so genuine. "I'll come, but it'll have to be early. About seven or so. I told Kieran I'd be back to see him at ten. They're releasing him."

Jack kissed her again, more gently. He was suddenly so glad that Amelia was on the other side of the guest house in her own room.

CHAPTER 11

She came to him, as she said she would. He was waiting for the text, and when she entered the lobby of the Inn, he took her hand silently and led her upstairs to his room. He sat on the edge of the bed and pulled her to him. He wrapped his arms around her waist, putting his head on her belly. He wanted to protect her. He wanted to crawl inside her.

Rose was on fire. All he had to do was touch her. She remembered the feel of him. His mouth on her breast, then deeper into her sex. The pulsing release and the earth shattering pleasure. He felt her arousal and gave a ragged breath, like he was fighting his response. She didn't have much experience in this department, but lust emboldened her. Lust and a stirring behind her ribs that made it all feel right. She ran a hand into his thick hair and pulled his head back. The lust in his eyes was like a fiery spear through her belly. He cupped her ass and pulled her astride him as he kissed her. He was hard and she moved along the ridge of him, headed for an explosion even fully clothed. He slid his hands up her rib cage until his thumbs found her nipples. He whipped her shirt off, unclasped her bra in front, and took her breasts in his hands. His mouth took long, warm pulls on her. "Jack!" She started moving up and down, hard.

"Rose," he grabbed her hips. "If you keep doing that I'm going to come." Jack had to get ahold of himself. He was losing control. He wanted inside her with a need that was going to turn him into an animal. He'd felt her. She was soft and wet and so tight. He flipped her on her back and started sliding her leggings off. Then he got on his knees, licking her right up the center. She cried out, but he was merciless. No teasing, no light touches. He sucked her flesh into his mouth like he was starved, and he was. Starved for her. She came so hard, it stole her voice. He slid a finger in so he could feel it. His cock pointing out that it could do the job much better. That she'd drive him wild and milk the life out of him. Then she was pulling his shoulders up.

"Jack, please. I need you. Come to me."

He went about his work again, and she made a garbled sound that told him she was so sensitive that he was going to have to peel her off the ceiling. "Jack, please." Her tone was harsher and he stopped. "I want you, Jack."

He leaned his head on her thigh, his breath tickling her sensitive flesh. "You have me."

She untangled herself and sat up on the bed. He was still clothed. "I don't want you to service me, Jack. I want you with me. I want to touch you. I want everything."

He stood, hands on his hips. He was wearing track pants and a Cambridge t-shirt. He looked delicious. His arousal was proud as it jutted out from his loose pants. Before he could protest, she put her hand on him. He dropped his head back and hissed. "Why are you holding back?" She asked as she stroked him, "Don't you like this?" He jerked his hips back, grabbing her wrists. His breathing was harsh, and she could tell she was getting to him. "Are you afraid I'll get you fired, Jack? A bit late for that, don't you think? Or do you really not want me? I mean, your body does, but maybe you don't…" He had her on her back in a flash. His tongue was deep in her mouth. He ground himself against her as he pinned her arms above her head.

"Every part of me wants you. Aches for you. How the hell can you doubt that for a minute?" The surge of their hips had Rose moaning his name.

To hell with it, Jack thought. He was done fighting this. Done with the wanting and denials. But he had a growing suspicion and knew that he couldn't take this any further until he and Rose talked. She'd never had a man pleasure her with his mouth, and what Amelia had told him about her being more innocent than she seemed made his conscience stand up and protest. He swallowed hard, his eyes searching. He pulled his hips away, trying to rein them both in so they could really talk. "Rose, I do want you but we can't take this any further until we talk." He rolled on his side, pulling her along so they were face to face. She looked confused. He asked, "Rose, are you a virgin?" It wasn't unheard of. Rare at her age, yes, but not impossible.

She hesitated, then shook her head. "No. I mean, not really." She stuttered over her words. "No, I'm not a virgin."

"That's usually an easy yes or no question. Please talk to me, Rose."

"I'm not a virgin. It's just been a really long time," she said, looking away.

He gently drew her face back to his. "How long?"

"Nine years." She said the words softly, flushing with embarrassment.

He thought about that, doing the math. "You were seventeen. Was it a schoolmate you were seeing?" He understood this. Young lads that age were rubbish between the sheets. Especially over eager ones.

"No, he was…a bit older. I was singing at a pub. I was barely seventeen but I lied about my age to get the job. He worked there as well, behind the bar."

Dread washed over Jack. "How much older?"

"I think about five or six years." A twenty-three year old man and she'd still been a teenage school girl. He tightened with suppressed anger.

"Rose, did he rape you?"

"No," she answered quickly. "I mean, he was my first and I agreed. I let him take me to his flat. I consented, but then," she swallowed. "We shouldn't be talking about this. I wouldn't want to hear about you with another woman."

"We need to talk about this, Rose. I know it's difficult, but we can't make love until I know I'm not going to hurt you. Did he take you to bed, then?"

She nodded, "Yes, he did. Only, it hurt. A lot more than I was expecting. He didn't do much to help me relax. He just got right down to it. It felt dreadful. I asked him to stop. You know, to ease up a bit." Jack cursed under his breath. "Anyway, he didn't. He just pushed harder. He told me it was too late to stop things now."

Jack touched her face so gently. "Rose, consent isn't a one-way door that locks after you go through it. The thing about consent is that it can be taken back at any point that you aren't comfortable. Especially if it's hurting you. He should have stopped. Hell, that bastard deserves to be in jail for even trying to take a seventeen year old to bed."

She shrugged. "It was a long time ago, Jack. I'm okay. Really."

"And after that? Did you have someone who treated you gently?" He knew, though. God, he almost wished the answer was different. That she'd had some young, age-appropriate lover. The typical fumbling of two inexperienced kids. Shagging her date in the backseat of a Volvo, sweating and panting and positive they'd love each other until they died. It was far from perfect, but it was better than some rotter bartender barreling through her body like a rapist.

"No, there wasn't anyone else. But that was my choice, Jack. So was going home with him. My choices, good or bad." He took a finger and traced a line from her temple to her chin, then he kissed her. She sighed and said, "You don't want to be with me now, do you?"

His eyes were sharp. "Of course I do. I just...I don't want it to be like this. I don't want to rush it."

She shook her head. "I can't believe you're going to just stop, Jack. That thing feels like a scud missile about to blow."

He barked out a laugh. "The Irish do have a way with words." He looked down at the offender in question as it jutted out. It did look rather ferocious. He laid down beside her, running a hand along her smooth thigh and over her hip. "There are other ways to give each other pleasure," he said. "And if you want to touch me, Rose, then I'd count myself a lucky man." Her face warmed at that. She pushed him on his back, kissing him and exploring his mouth.

"I liked watching you in the shower," she said a little hoarsely. "I think you're beautiful Jack. I want to make you feel as good as you've made me feel. I need it. I may not be experienced, but I'm no saint and I'm not that young girl anymore. I want this." As she said it, she slipped his t-shirt off. She looked over his tight abs and broad chest and his thick, muscular biceps. "I want to do more than touch you, Jack. I want to do to you what you did to me." He hissed as his hips jerked, and she took that as a yes. She eased his pants down, taking him in her hand.

His voice was strained. "I want to take you home, Rose. I want to make love in that big bed overlooking London. I want your first time to be perfect."

"It won't be my first time," she said, daring him to argue.

He wasn't sure about that, but he said, "Call it a do-over." Then he groaned. "That feels incredible."

She moved before she lost her nerve, working on pure instinct as she moved down his body and took him in her mouth. A surge of power went through her as he voiced his passion. He was at her mercy, and it felt so right, being the one to give him pleasure. It was delicious.

* * *

ROSE LEFT BEFORE AMELIA WOKE. Jack finally went down the corridor to her room, and when she answered, she was still in her sleeping garments. It was a tank top and shorts, and that's the first time he ever had a stab of fear pierce through him about his sister. She was so thin, her bones jutted from her skin. And she looked so tired. She was physically exhausted. His face was stricken. The corner of her mouth turned up. "That bad, is it?"

"Amelia, my love. What have you done to yourself?" She opened the door, giving him an indulgent look. He put a hand up. "Don't, Amelia. Don't start with the appeasing words and comments about how I don't understand the dance world." He bit back his harsh tone, closing the door. His eyes held pain, and that's when she finally let the wall down. The tears were quiet. He held her softly, afraid she'd break.

"It's not what you think. I swear it. I'm not anorexic. This dieting and training was not my idea. My teacher…"

"The one from the university? I'll have his balls on a fucking plate!" he growled.

She shook her head. "No, he was against it. He's kind of a bastard, but this was a bit much for even him. But he couldn't argue with the results, so he let it go."

"Which teacher?"

"The private one mother hired." She put on a brave face. "I agreed to the arrangement. It's not all on her. She did what I asked. She reached out to the ballet community, and to some old contacts. Supposedly this woman is the best."

"The best at what? Making you look like an emaciated twelve year old? Christ, Amelia." She went over and put a sweatshirt on, blushing. "Jesus, sweetheart I'm sorry. You know I think you're the most beautiful girl in the world." He took her shoulders in his hands. "Don't ever hide from me. It's why you came to me, right? You came to me instead of going home, because you knew I'd protect you. Even if it's from yourself." Her chin wobbled and she just nodded her head.

"You're going to take a medical leave from school. You can't be around that community. You're also going to be seen by a doctor. This can't continue. You have more to give the world than your dancing. You know that deep down. It'll be a few short years and potentially damage your body forever. You know I'm right."

"I don't want to go to some doctor just to have him tell me to eat more. I know I need to eat more. I can't just leave school!"

"You can. Please, Amelia, do this for me. At least talk to Rose. She's a nurse. Maybe she has a doctor here that can fit you in today. Just for a few tests."

She thought on it. "Then mother might not find out."

"Forget mother! She's never had balance in her life. She's trying to make you into this image of her. I remember father telling me that mother's ballet career had been short. A few minor parts in major ballets. And the reason she pushed you when you were young was because she blamed her parents. They'd not committed. Hadn't gotten her private teachers and helped her be the best. She's trying to relive those days for herself. Not for you."

"Why do you hate her so much, Jackson?"

He closed his eyes. "I don't hate her, Amelia. I just…" He searched for the right words. His feelings about his mother were complicated. "She wasn't a very good mother. Sure, she wasn't abusive, but she was cold and distant. Uninvolved unless it made her status in the community better. Always pushing, never giving us what really mattered. I got more love from Judith than I ever did from her."

Amelia smiled at that. "Tea and biscuits, then a kiss on the nose and off to bed."

He nodded. "And she listens. She is present. Like father was."

"I miss him," she said softly. "And Louie." Her eyes closed as her pain overwhelmed her. "Our numbers are dwindling."

"Then we'll have to make sure to take care of each other. And we'll find new numbers."

"Like Rose?" she asked, not teasing.

"Rose and I are complicated."

Amelia said, "I know that you've never looked at anyone the way you look at her. And I know she's got a beautiful heart. She's had it hard, but she made a family out of what they had left."

"Just like you and me," he said softly.

ROSE SAT in the exam room with Amelia as the doctor spoke with her. Jesus wept. She'd had no idea how thin Amelia was. She had a tight, flat stomach and lean muscle, but she was dangerously underweight. She hadn't had a period in two years. Rose and the doctor felt that there was no underlying psychological diagnosis. This wasn't an eating disorder. This was some very bad advice from two women who should have known better. Rose couldn't believe the girl's mother had encouraged this. She thought of her brother, trying like hell to gain weight and keep meat on his bones before the chemo started.

The doctor's brows were drawn. "Your body fat is too low for a woman in her reproductive years. I know that this is common in athletes and in the ballet world, but given the stress fractures, it's obvious that the weight loss hasn't had the desired effect." The doctor put her arm on Amelia's shoulder. "Despite the calcium supplements, the lack of Vitamin D and the anemia have taken a toll on your body. Have you ever fainted at home or at rehearsal?"

Amelia nodded. "Just twice. The teacher said to take iron pills, but with no food in my stomach…"

"You threw them up?" the doctor asked, although she knew the answer. Amelia nodded. The doctor said, "Your teacher is a stupid cow." Amelia choked on a laugh. "Now, if you're comfortable, I'm going to let Nurse Tierney get back to her brother's discharge paperwork. I'm going to give you a pelvic to make sure nothing else is going on with those menstrual cycles. Then you and I are going to talk about how to get you back up to fighting shape. Given the old fractures on you right foot, as well as the new ones, your dance career needs to be put on hold for at least six months. You're going to eat, take a different cycle of supplements, and you're going to cool it on the exercise. I'm officially going to prescribe Netflix, cheeseburgers, and a bit of whiskey on a regular basis."

"Whiskey?" Amelia asked. She looked at Rose, who was laughing as she listened to the exchange.

"Aye, whiskey. You English girls need to lighten up."***

Rose came into the room and saw her granny folding up the last of Kieran's clothing. She put it in the bag, then a book he'd been reading. Her brother was on the edge of the bed, and Jack was texting someone. He put his phone away. "How is she?"

Kieran looked sharply. "Who? What's wrong?" Then it hit him. "Jack, where is your sister?"

"She was just under the weather. She'll be fine. Let's get this bag to the car and get you out of here. Eh?" Kieran narrowed his eyes, but decided that it probably wasn't any of his business.

Amelia met them in the lobby and then Rose said her goodbyes. "I love you. I know you don't understand, but I have to go back. It'll only be another week at the most. Then I'll be home for good."

Her grandmother leaned in for a goodbye embrace. "I know where you've been and why."

Rose met her eyes for an intense moment. "I never could fool you. You'll hear it all soon enough, but later. This isn't finished." Her granny just nodded, knowing that her granddaughter was just as stubborn as she was. Just as stubborn as her mother had been.

Jack's jaw tightened. *Home for good.* She'd leave him in less than a week. He should insist she stay here, but he wanted more time with her. And he knew that she had to do this. She had to go back to London and back in time. She had to retrace the steps of her six year old self and see if she could do something to help her mother. And she'd not finished with Mick Tierney either. The thing about parents was, they didn't have to be good parents in order for you to love them. Look at Amelia and his mother.

JACK DROPPED his sister off at his flat in Battersea, as she'd be staying with him. With Rose involved with the club, he couldn't let her stay in the house with Rose, in case someone had a mind to follow her home from work. Rose didn't know that he'd also put a tail on her. He wasn't taking any chances with someone getting wise to why she was still hanging around. They still had a killer to catch, not to mention the general low character of Luce's associates.

It wasn't a question of him following her inside. He was like a moth. Drawn to her light. He wasn't going to fight it anymore. He was going to savor the time they had left. Fuck this case, fuck Nigel, fuck his traitorous heart that would be wrecked after this. All he wanted was Rose. He was going to take the rest of this day. Nigel and Katherine didn't even know he was back. He watched her take the bag off her shoulder, stretching her neck. He put his keys on the bureau by the door. It was almost like a husband coming home to his wife. He didn't say a word. He just went to her and picked her up off the ground. His eyes never left her as he ascended the stairs. She was wearing a dress. A pretty green dress that flowed around her knees. The v neckline showed her pale neck and accented her slender face. He'd never seen her in heels. He knew she'd done it for him. No boots or leather. No false identities. This was Rose as he might see her heading to mass or out for drinks with her friends. It was a gift she was giving him.

He put her down by the bed. Then he sat, bringing her to him. "Rose. Please tell me you want this."

She took his hand and ran it up her smooth thigh, underneath the silkiness of her dress. His breath caught. He brought the other hand up, feeling her silky panties. He knew what was under there. White skin, round hips and a perfect ass. The auburn triangle of hair that shrouded her secret flesh. He took one hand and slid between her thighs. The silk was damp, and he knew how slippery she'd be underneath. He found the small spot that was the center of her passion. He thumbed it and she moaned.

He had to have a taste. Before he slipped inside her and it was over too fast. He slid her panties off, taking one leg and stretching it up so that her foot was on the bed next to him. Then he was under that skirt, pulling her hips tight against his mouth. She was totally uninhibited, staying against his skillful mouth as she came. She screamed his name and choked on it as he wrung the last bit of sensation from her. Then her knees gave out and he guided her to the bed.

He undressed her slowly, then himself. She was flushed and glassy eyed and so ready for him. But he was worried about hurting her. "Rose, straddle my hips." He was at the headboard now, lying on that big bed, hard as rock and aching for her. "I want you on top. I want you to be able to control this. Ease yourself into it. It'll hurt less." She sobered at that, looking unsure. "Nothing you do will be wrong." He let out a ragged breath. "I've never been so turned on. You are exquisite. You'll be able to take me Rose. If you go slow, you can take all of me, and you are going to love it."

He rolled a condom on, then took her wrist and pulled her gently. She was so beautiful. He looked up at her and smiled. "Take me, Rose. Take all the time you need."

Rose looked down at his hard chest, feeling the tip of that long length right at her core. A little moan escaped as she looked down between them. He would fit. She knew it. This worked, and it didn't have to hurt. She was getting her do-over, and she was going to like it this time. She saw the sheen on his mouth and thought about how shamelessly she'd taken her pleasure against his mouth. It emboldened her. She stood him up and felt that velvety tip begin to part her slick heat. Her body instinctively resisted, but all she had to do was look at him. He watched greedily where their bodies were joined, fighting to hold himself back. Struggling not to try and push her down or thrust up. She was so sensitive and ready, and suddenly it wasn't scary. A little pain could be delicious. So she held him in her hand and lowered herself, feeling that sweet sting of stretching. She heard his breath stutter. "Such control. Is it hard to stay still, Jack? Is it hard not taking what you want?"

"You are an evil tease. I love it. Go as slowly as you like. Slay me with it, Rose." His sultry voice made her hips jerk and she pushed down harder, taking more. She found a rhythm, gaining more with every push.

Jack looked between them as she impaled herself slowly. She was tight, but she was wet and ready, and she slowly found her confidence. Then it happened. Their hips met. "I'm in you, Rose." His voice shook like a boy's.

She smiled so sweetly it nearly undid him. "I'm so full, I can't tell who is who. There's no space between us." His heart shattered. She went up, then took him again. She was so beautiful. Her nipples were flushed as she arched and rode him, her breaths coming short. She lowered herself and took his mouth, kissing him deeply. Then she said against his lips, "Jack, I want you on top."

"Are you sure?"

"I trust you. Show me, Jack. Show me it doesn't have to hurt. You don't have to hold back. I want Jackson De Clare undiluted." His eyes flared and he flipped her on her back. She squealed.

"Be careful what you ask for." Her eyes widened as he pulled his hips back, rolling them as he filled her. She gasped, her hands shooting to his ass. "You like that? You want more?" She moaned as he filled her, deep and slow. He cupped her ass and lifted her hips, going deeper. "I dreamed of this, Rose. I wanted this so desperately. To look down at you. At those liquid brown eyes as I filled you. As you came in my arms." He quickened his pace, thrusting deep. "Tell me if it's too much."

Her neck arched, "Don't stop," she said on a whimper. Her

eyes were desperate, begging for him to show her, begging for that sweet release where he'd see into her soul. He felt it start. "Jack." She was begging.

"Let go, Rose. Take me with you."

Rose had experienced an orgasm before, but this was very different. He was a dominating presence in her body that she didn't want to let go. She felt her body answer him, pulling at him, and that's when she hit the ceiling. She screamed so loud, it rang through the room. Jack thrust into the storm, and she felt him lose the grip on himself. The smell of him and the taste of his skin. The solid fact of him as she clung to his shoulders. It was overwhelming. Both not enough and too much, and a swirl of sensation that left them both ruined and reborn in equal measure.

Jack always used condoms, but for the first time in his life, he resented the presence between them. He wanted skin on skin. Feeling her release snapped his control; the white flash of pleasure blinding him until he felt like he might die from it. The French called it *the little death,* but there was nothing little about this joining. A piece of him would indeed die when Rose left him. He held her as they both trembled, and he knew he'd never be the same.

CHAPTER 12

*J*ack looked down at Rose, asleep on her stomach. She was resplendent in the city lights. The sun went down early as winter was approaching. He looked over the city and never wanted this day to end. But he had two bits of business. He had to see his mother. He was going to have it out with her, and then he was going to pack up several boxes of Amelia's belongings and have the staff drive it over to Battersea. He had an entire bedroom open just for her. He was going to start taking care of his sister.

Then he was going to go see Luce and act like nothing had happened. Play the stupid barfly who liked to hang out like a poser in a biker club. He was going to do his goddamn job. Because he wanted this over. He wanted Rose out of the city, even though it was going to kill him. He wanted her safe. She had her own responsibilities. Kieran needed her at home. The boy had a tough road ahead of him, and he needed his strong, intelligent, loyal sister. Once you got past the arrogance of youth and his distaste for Englishman, he was a likable young man. What twenty year old man wasn't a bit arrogant? And given his history with the father, it was no wonder he didn't care for some Londoner in a slick suit sniffing around his sister.

He thought about how he'd spent the day and his body stirred. Rose was everything he thought she'd be and more. He'd had her four times, looking up as she rode him, then watching her back arch and her hips tip up as he took her from behind. They'd finally drifted off, and he'd curled into her, smelling her hair and tasting the skin on her shoulder. They'd lain in sleepy contentment. The last time had been so slow and tender, the thought of it made his eyes burn. He'd never experienced such intense pleasure mixed with such raw emotion .

He'd bedded a lot of women. He wasn't proud of it, but he liked sex. He had needs. And he wasn't interested in women who had wedding bells ringing in their ears. The truth was, that in all the years he'd been having sex, it had been nothing more than recreational. He'd been fond of the women, but he hadn't loved any of them. The women in his social circles who weren't looking for a husband were a bit cold. They liked the mutual pleasure. They like to take the edge off with a big man who knew how to throw them down and fuck them properly. He was a skilled lover, and he knew how to please a woman. But this day with Rose had been a revelation. He'd trembled in her arms, for fuck sake. Her pleasure had fed his soul. And in those hours with her, he'd felt a part of something beautiful.

He turned down the drive of his mother's Chelsea estate dreading this blow-out and understanding it was inevitable. He cut through the kitchen, Judith giving him a motherly hug. "You look better now that you've shaved. I missed this darling face." Judith rubbed a hand over his hair. The chilly female voice came from behind. "Judith, we'll require the white burgundy with the evening meal." She looked at Jack speculatively. "Jackson, I don't think I've ever seen your hair so unkempt. Please, join us for dinner."

"Us?" he asked.

"Yes. Your sister has come this evening. I sent a car for her."

He almost groaned. Dammit. Why was his sister so weak when it came to his mother? So eager to please. "I think that's a good idea. We have much to discuss, Mother."

Amelia gave him a sheepish look as he entered the dining room. "Hello, love. I'm surprised to see you here. I thought you were going to take a nap?"

"Mother called, and..." She looked at her mother, a flush coming up her pale neck.

"Amelia, darling. Do sit up straight. Now, Jackson, what is this I hear about Amelia living with you? Surely you understand that's unacceptable. Her dormitory fees are paid for the semester and she's mid-term. I've spoken with her instructors."

"Mother, Amelia needs to take medical leave from her schooling. She's unwell."

His mother waved a hand, "Oh, Jackson. Don't be dramatic. She'll rest the injury for two weeks, then cut back on rehearsals for another four. I've spoken with her private instructor."

"You mean the stupid cow who encouraged her to starve herself half to death and dance on an injured foot? I don't think so, Mother. You will not continue to bully her into a career that's hurting her. I won't stand for it!"

"Do not raise your voice, Jackson. I am the head of this family."

"Bang up fucking job you're doing. Louie is dead and she's in a cast. What do you have in store for me?"

His mother sucked in a breath and Amelia stood abruptly.

"Stop it! Both of you! I am not a child. Stop talking about me as if I'm not in the room!"

"Amelia, sit down. This is completely inappropriate. I did not raise either of you to speak to your mother with such disrespect." She stifled her next words as the kitchen staff brought in the first course. He watched as a bowl of broth was put in front of Amelia, then looked down at the creamy soup he'd been given. His mother said, "Judith, no cheese or croutons on the salad, and vinegar only."

He shook his head. "Are you actually having Judith alter Amelia's meals? Are you serious? Judith, bring my sister out the same thing you brought me."

When his mother gave Judith a nasty glare, he said. "Actually, Judith, I would love if you'd pack up the meal for us to take home. Could you do that? We aren't staying and I don't want all of your effort to go to waste."

His sister sighed, shoving the broth away. His mother said, "I assure you, her diet is approved by a dietician. You are overreacting. Stop this nonsense and let us have a civil meal."

"Are you actually going to feed all of us or are you planning on bringing her a bowl of ice chips for dessert?" His mother's steely glare lasted a moment, then she nodded at the cook. Judith took the broth and went back to the kitchen.

Amelia said, "Now, if you'll both kindly shut your gobs, I'll tell you what my plans are." Jack choked on a laugh, because he knew where she'd picked up that little term. "I'm taking the rest of the semester off. I'll return in the spring session, but I will not return to dance until at least the summer session. That is if my doctor approves it."

"I've spoken with your doctor," her mother said coolly.

Amelia slapped the table, which both shocked and delighted Jack. "You have no right to speak to my doctor. I am an adult. I could report him to the medical board. Instead

I'm going to fire him. I have a new doctor. One that was recommended by a physician I saw in Belfast yesterday."

"Belfast? Why on earth were you in that dreadful city, and why would you see a doctor there?" Her mother's tone was incredulous.

Oh shit, thought Jack. *Don't tell her about Rose.*

"We went to see a friend in the hospital. Jack's friend Rose has a brother…"

"Amelia, we don't need to get into the particulars." Jack sent her a warning glance which didn't escape his mother.

"An Irish friend? A woman? What's this, Jackson? Is she a colleague from work?"

Amelia sent him an apologetic look. Jack went on the defense. "I'm not here to talk about that. Amelia will pack a few bags after dinner, then she's moving to my guest room. I'll have the staff bring over anything else she needs." This was altering his plans, because he was supposed to be going to the club, but he wasn't leaving Amelia here.

His mother tightened her hand in a fist, reining in her temper. "That isn't necessary. She has a room upstairs. Or maybe you're forgetting who pays for her expensive education and private lessons?"

"Actually, father did, and as you know, he left me as executor of our estate when I turned twenty-three. You are a figurehead. If you try to press your will in this matter, I will start making changes to how I run the family affairs. Starting with downsizing you to a smaller estate. One woman does not need a house this big or such a large staff."

His mother gasped. "I don't know what has gotten into you, Jackson. Your father would be ashamed of you." That stung, but not the way she'd meant it to.

"You're correct, mother. I was the oldest. I should have intervened with Louie before he got so out of hand. I should have been more involved with Amelia. That changes tonight.

She lives with me. I have more than enough room. Now, shall we eat whatever gorgeous meal Judith has prepared and end this discussion? I'm tiring of it." Judith looked like a deer in the headlights as she stood with a platter of food, waiting to serve them.

The meal was tense and in the end his mother dismissed herself to make a phone call. Amelia went up to pack her bags, and he went to the kitchen to speak with Judith. "Can I borrow your car again? My jag won't hold very much."

"Would you like me to just follow you, Jackson? I don't mind."

Amelia spoke from behind them. "Jack, didn't you have to work tonight? Why don't you just let Judith take me? Then we can swing by the townhouse and take Rose a plate. She must be exhausted." Jack liked that idea, but he wasn't sure they should involve Judith in the Rose predicament. He didn't want his mother anywhere near her.

On cue, his mother walked into the kitchen. "Must you all gather in the kitchen? We have a drawing room."

Amelia stifled a giggle. Her mother was so uptight, and who the hell called it a drawing room anymore? She said, "We were just leaving, Mother. Judith is going to drive me to Battersea. Jackson has a meeting. It was good to see you." She walked over to her mother who turned her face to receive an impersonal kiss to the cheek. Jackson suddenly wished Granny Keirsty would adopt them.

ROSE WALKED into Luce's club well rested and determined. Her time with Jack had been so beautiful. She felt changed, somehow. She knew it wasn't permanent, and that simple fact made her terribly sad when she dwelled on it too long. But she wouldn't undo it, and she was so very grateful that she'd been able to experience the sort of fulfilling intimacy that changed the way a person looked at sexuality. That aside, she had a life to get back to. Her brother's chemo started soon. So, it was time to push herself.

Her steps slowed for a moment when she saw her father standing by a billiards table. She wasn't sure she'd ever get used to the sight of him. He'd been a memory for so long, it was hard to meet him face to face. He said something quiet to one of the other men, handing off his pool cue. Then he approached her. "Rose, how was your trip?"

He was so easy going, it confounded her. She knew he was trying a new tactic. Coming off like he was letting her have the control. Or maybe it was for the benefit of the other men. A display of familial strife could erode his authority.

"It was fine, Da. I need to work."

"I heard about your crash. Where are you staying? Do you need money?"

"Gran needs money. Send it to her. She barely gets by."

He led her over to a far off booth. "Please, Rose. You prefer Rose, right? Please just sit and talk with me for a few minutes. Luce won't mind."

She sat across from him, silent. He said, "Look, I know things have been tight. I didn't realize how tight things were, or I would have tried to send more money. I'm sorry. I don't bring in large wages. I sent what I could, but I'll start sending more. Kieran's going to need things, and he's going to school now. I'll send more."

"Crime isn't paying like it used to?" she said snidely.

"I don't take any money from those dealings. That's not my function here. You may judge me for turning a blind eye to it, and I suppose you have good reason, but I never profited from it. I make money working on the bikes and cars when I have the time. I'm no pimp and I'm no drug dealer."

"Then why do you stay, Da?"

"It's not a life that you come and go as you please." That's all he said, but she understood. M.C.s of this nature, the one percenters, were not so easy to walk away from. "And at the time, I felt like I owed them. When your mother died," he clenched his jaw, and she suddenly remembered that scene in the kitchen.

She reached over before she lost her courage. She put her hand over his. "I remember. At least, I'm starting to. You were trying to give Kieran a bottle. He was crying for Mammy." She watched a tremor go through her father. "But we needed you, Da. Ye left us when we needed you most. Kieran never even knew you." She took her hand away, angry with herself. "He's a good lad. Smart and strong. You missed it, Da. You missed everything."

"I couldn't keep you with me, Rose. And your granny lost her daughter. If she took you in, it was like a second chance for her. Having a bit of Annalise back in her home. She was so angry. She blamed me for her death, but I knew she'd keep you safe. She moved out of Belfast and got that cottage in Ballyclare just for you, but I couldn't stay."

The words were unspoken, the doubts he had about what had happened, but she saw them on his face. He looked around. "It's best if you go."

"I won't. Not until I remember. I hid her away. If I'd been braver or been strong enough to face the memories, then maybe things would have been different."

"No, love. I won't hear it. You were scarcely more than a babe yourself. If you saw something, I'll never forgive myself. I shouldn't have left that weekend."

Rose felt a prickling on her neck and turned to look across the bar. Hammer and Luce were both watching them. "I need to get to work. Just be careful, Da."

* * *

LUCE SAT NEXT TO MICK, eyes assessing him. "I need to know what went on. I've given you time, Mick. I've given you my trust. Now it's time to tell me everything."

Mick exhaled, then lit a cigarette. He snapped his lighter closed and blew away from Luce. "They have nothing on me. They grabbed the wrong man for all that. You know as well as I do I had nothing to tell them. I stay out of that shit. I don't want any part of it. And after that kid overdosed outside the club, I'm stunned you still have the stomach for it."

"That was an isolated mistake."

Mick took a drag on his fag and said, "Well, I'm not so sure about that. They put a file in front of me four inches thick. All overdoses in the last six months. They think it's coming from your house but they can't prove it."

Luce's jaw was tight. "Fucking crikey. Do you think they made the whole thing up?"

"Don't know. The question is, do you take Hammer's word for it? This isn't the first time he's had a little side action going that you didn't know about or approve."

Luce rubbed his face. "I hate that shit. I never wanted to get into drugs. Guns were necessary, profitable. The whores are good for morale. My boys are their best customers and no one gets out of line. The drugs, though...I'm thinking of pulling back on that. It's bad business. Louie was kind of a tosser. Too fucking eager, but he wasn't a bad lad. It was unfortunate," he said with regret.

"Don't you ever miss the old days, when it was more about riding with your mates and less about money? Fuck me, Luce. When's the last time you closed this place up and did a real ride? Remember when we used to drive through the Cotswolds and scare the fuck out of the locals?" Luce cracked off a laugh at that. "All the while, their girls giving us a wink. What was that baker's wife's name again?"

Luce smiled, "Gwendolyn. Fair curls and a fine, round ass." He rubbed his lip. "I'd forgotten about that weekend. It's when you and Annalise told us..." he caught himself, shutting down the memory.

"That we were pregnant. We were going to have a baby." The longing in Mick's voice was palpable.

Luce looked over at Rose and his face fell. "That seems like a lifetime ago. Christ, our little Rosebud."

"I see the way you look at her, brother. She's my daughter." His voice held warning.

Luce just nodded, taking a pull on his beer. "She's beautiful, but you're right. She's not for the likes of me. She needs someone younger. A better man." As if on cue, Jack walked through the front door.

"Who the fuck is that bloke? Is she seeing him?"

"I don't know. I think something's going on, but they don't advertise. He's a good lad and he watches out for her."

Mick said, "What does he do for a living? That bike he rides is top shelf."

"I don't know. He's private like. But he's a good sort, I think. Minds his own business most of the time, unless it has to do with her."

"I don't like him."

Luce just smiled at that. "Careful, old friend. She'll not thank you for trying to play the protective Da. It's been too long."

"Aye, she's stubborn like her mother," Mick grumbled.

Luce cracked off another laugh. "You mean like her Da! For feck sake, Mick. She's a sharp-tongued Tierney to the bone." Now Mick was smiling. Kinda made a man proud. He put an arm on his shoulder, closing the distance over the table. "It's good to have you back, brother."

* * *

ROSE WAS in rare form tonight, and Jack knew what she was about. She worked the room like a proper cocktail waitress, chatting it up with all of the club members. Going to them instead of them coming to the bar or shouting out their orders. Getting to know them. Hearing their voices. Now that they knew who she was, they opened up a bit too. Talking about her father like he was a choir boy among a den of wolves. He was surprised when Luce stood up on a chair and whistled. "Attention my fallen sons! It's come to my attention that I've become a boring old bastard, and have been neglecting Boudicca." Jack knew that the Celtic warrior queen, Boudicca, had been the inspiration for Luce naming his bike. "The club closes at midnight." The moans rolled through the crowd.

"How the bloody hell does that make you more fun?"

"Excellent question ye fat bastard. You're all going to go home, get a decent night's sleep, and report here at half ten in the morning. We're taking a ride through the Cotswolds and all the way to the Welsh coast. I've gotta see a baker's wife about a muffin."

Rose's eyes shot to her father's as he barked out a harsh laugh, then bent over, holding in a belly laugh. He was so handsome. His brown eyes gleamed, and suddenly she was five years old. The memory rode over her conscious mind. She was in this very club, and five year old Rose had just stunned the crowd of bikers and her parents by saying...

"Uncle Luce called the lad that brings the ale a stupid twat. What's a twat?" Her father was in stitches.

Her mother was caught between anger and trying not to laugh. She speared Luce with a look, and he had the good sense to look contrite. "Sorry, Annalise. I didn't see her come in. He dropped an entire case in the back room!" he said in his defense.

Her father had picked her up, kissing her forehead. "That's a naughty word, Rosie. You can't be saying that anymore."

"But Uncle Luce says it."

Luce spoke then. "Uncle Luce is naughty as well. I didn't have a good mammy like you. No one taught me how to speak like a good lad. I've got terrible manners. You listen to your mammy. She'll teach ye how to be a lady."

"Like an old lady? Like the women who ride on the back of your bike?"

The three of them spoke in unison, "No!" Luce said, "Christ no, love. Like a proper lady. Smart and sweet. You're our little Rosebud. We expect grand things from our girl." Then he brushed her hair away from her face and kissed her on the temple.

Rose came back to the present and was smiling through tears. Luce met her eyes and approached slowly. "What is it, love?"

"You called the man who delivered the ale a stupid twat."

He cocked his head and then he remembered. He laughed. A deep belly laugh that lit up his face. "And did you ever use that word again?" His eyes were playful.

She smiled, "Not until thirty-seconds ago. Some moments make an impression, I suppose."

She watched old pain wash over him. "Your mother would be proud. I'll be sorry to see you go, sweet Rose, but this is no place for you."

"Does that mean I'm not invited on the ride?" Rose asked with her hands on her hips.

"You're absolutely invited. But that bike of yours will never make it to Wales and back. New tires or not. And you don't have a windshield. You'll have to ride with your Da," he gave her a devilish grin that was almost handsome. "Unless you'd rather ride with me?"

"I'll volunteer. I've got a sissy bar I can clip to the back tonight." Jack inserted himself in the conversation. "Unless this is club only?"

161

Rose bristled. "I don't need a sissy bar." But both men ignored her.

Then her father was there. "She rides with me."

"Excuse me?" she said. This territorial thing was getting old.

Luce just smiled and said to Jack. "I don't see why not. As for the lass, it's her decision who she rides with."

"Thank you, Luce, but that was never in question. Now if you're all done puffing your bloody chests out, I need to start washing beer glasses."

* * *

JACK TURNED the key and felt his heart racing with anticipation. He opened the door and there she was. Some women might have put on a bit of lingerie. Not Rose. She knew just how to get to him. She put her glass of water down on the counter and leaned a hand on the granite. She had those come hither eyes and was dressed in nothing but his oversized Cambridge t-shirt. Her smooth, toned legs were bare and beautiful. He crossed the distance in three strides, then his mouth was on hers. She coiled a hand in his hair, the other one around his shoulder. He cupped her ass and lifted her off the ground, and her legs came around his waist.

Rose moaned as Jack pushed her back to the wall. He was so beautiful. Like a big cat coming after her, predatory and sleek. She loved his hands on her, urgent and firm. He'd been gentle with her the first few times time, showing her that he could be. But this was about pure male dominance. Lust and hunger swirling around them as he ground his hips against her.

"Rose, I need you. Fuck! I can't wait!"

She rolled her hips against him, answering his plea. He fumbled with his jeans, freeing himself. Then she felt the rip of her panties as he pulled them aside. He thumbed the top of her sex as he slid into her, and they both cried out.

Rose was close to climaxing as he sheathed himself deep inside her. He was hard and warm as he started to move. Something was different. She moaned at the feel of him. It hadn't felt this good the first... She froze. He came to the same startling reality as she did. "Jesus, Rose. I'm sorry." He retreated as he said it.

He put her down and he was shaking from unspent lust. "They're upstairs."

They ascended the stairs hand in hand, and Jack was livid with himself for such a stupid, selfish mistake. He'd forgotten to put on a condom. He took her to the bed and she put a hand on his face. "It's okay. I didn't think of it either. I'm not ovulating. I think we stopped in time. It was only a few moments."

They both knew it could happen, however. It only took one eager swimmer. If he were to get her pregnant, that would uncomplicate everything, wouldn't it? He'd quit the goddamn job and drag her down the aisle. He was startled to realize that the idea of marrying Rose and having a family with her didn't scare the ever-loving shit out of him. He'd only known her a couple of weeks, but some things didn't take a lot of time to realize. He didn't take his eyes from hers. He just handed her the condom and watched with intense pleasure as she rolled it on him. Then he kissed her, splitting her thighs over his cock. Heaven. She was heaven.

* * *

HE LEFT after a couple of hours, needing to get ready for the road trip. He hated leaving town, but this ride could be more than it seemed. The agency knew there was a connection in Wales.

He willed himself to get some rest, knowing that an all-day motorcycle ride was going to take some energy. With Rose on the back of his bike, he had to stay sharp. He missed her. He'd just seen her an hour ago, and he longed to have her next to him. To put his nose in her silky mane and smell the back of her neck. Suddenly, the thought of having Rose wrapped around him, driving through the countryside didn't seem like work.

CHAPTER 13

*R*ose ran to the front door, surprised that Jack was so early. She knew he had an early morning meeting. She heard the key turn in the lock and was startled to see a petite, elegantly dressed woman walk in like she owned the place. Her face was tense and Rose had the fleeting idea that she looked like an older version of Amelia.

Rose straightened her spine, suddenly very aware of her leather accessories and faded jeans. "Excuse me, can I help you?"

"I'm not sure you can. I was expecting to find my son at home, or perhaps my daughter." The woman's tone was calculating, and Rose felt sure that this little early morning visit was for her, not Jack. "May I have the pleasure of your name?"

"I'm Rose Tierney. I'm a friend of Jack's. I'm surprised, being their mother, that you're not aware. He moved to Battersea. Amelia is there with him."

She raised a brow, letting her score the point. "And how did you come to be living here?" She gave Rose a head-to-toe appraisal, stopping at her scuffed boots.

"Is there something I can help you with? I have a busy morning, but I can call your son if that's what you need."

"What do you do in Ireland? Rose, was it?"

"Yes. I've just graduated from nursing school."

"Ah, well university can be expensive. So, why don't we dispense with the niceties and have a candid conversation." Rose raised a brow, crossing her arms over her abdomen. She continued, unwilling to acknowledge Rose's irritation. "My son is a good man. Too good, some might say. It's obvious he's taken you into his home out of some misplaced desire to do the honorable thing, but I can tell you that you are not the sort of woman with whom he normally entangles himself. I think it would be best for everyone if you went back to whatever Belfast crevice you came from." She took an envelope out of her bag. "This should cover some of your student expenses as well as transportation back across the sea. Perhaps a new pair of boots." She glanced down and Rose flushed with anger.

"Who in the bloody hell do you think you are? You know nothing about me. And it's quite obvious that your children got the best of their traits from their father. Now get out."

"Miss Tierney, my son is in line for a barony. Whatever he is getting out of this arrangement will not be worth his reputation in the end. He will grow bored with slumming it and send you on your way once he's done with you. I'm offering you the opportunity to bow out gracefully with a bit of pocket money for your troubles." The jab hit its mark. Rose had always known this was destined to fail. They were too different. But she wasn't going to give this woman the satisfaction of knowing she got to her.

"If he's going to recycle me back to Ireland, then you have no reason to be concerned. Now take that envelope with you before I decide to forget my manners. Goodbye, Mrs. De Clare."

JACK RUBBED his eyes with his thumb and index finger. Nigel said, "I don't like you being that far out with no back up."

"Nigel, let me do my job. Luce trusts me. He sees nothing more than a pretty boy who likes to hang with the bad boys. He thinks my main objective is Rose."

"Is it?"

"Fuck off, Nigel," he said smoothly. "There's a GPS on my bike and on my cell phone. This could be important."

Nigel sighed. "Okay, just watch your ass, Jackson. After this case is over, we need you back at your old job and I don't want to train someone else."

"Aren't you sentimental," Jack said with a smirk.

Katherine piped in from behind him. "Don't believe it for a moment. He's an insensitive bastard." She handed Nigel a mug of tea. "And he's buying me lunch for this, because normally I don't fetch tea. I'm of the *get up and get it your fucking self* generation." Both men threw back their heads and laughed.

* * *

THE DAY WAS GLORIOUS. One of those rare, sunny autumn days in England that made you remember why you lived here. Jack loved the feel of Rose behind him, her auburn strands whipping from underneath her helmet. She'd worn her old one, and he knew that it was more to feel some sort of connection to the past. To her mother. She was distant, though. And he wondered if something was bothering her. Maybe the incident with the condom, or the lack of one in this case.

Rose closed her eyes, nestling into the leather and strength and the male heat of Jack. Or Jackson as his family called him. Jackson De Clare who came from old money and was in line for a barony. Jackson De Clare who was playing a role instead of living his suit and tie lifestyle. Was she part of that game? She knew that what happened between them in the bedroom was genuine. She may not be an expert, but she knew that his passion for her was real, against his better judgment. She always assumed that was due to the job he was doing. Maybe she'd been wrong. *He'll grow bored with slumming it...* Damn. That one had stung. She wasn't some gutter rat, despite how he'd found her. She came from a modest, working class neighborhood, but her family was not and never would be considered slumming it. She thought of her brother, so smart and handsome. He'd been so strong, too. His physical form had dwindled rapidly from the onset of the leukemia, and he hated it. Once an athlete, tall and long limbed, and murder walking on the rugby field. She needed to end this and go home. After this ride, she'd let herself have the weekend, and then she'd leave. This was no place for her. She didn't belong in her father's world, and she didn't belong in Jack's.

Jack felt Rose tense behind him. He patted her hands that were gathered around his waist, and took a peek in the rear view mirror. Her eyes were closed. He could see it through her clear goggles. And her face showed pain. Sorrow. Jesus... she was leaving. He burned underneath his sternum, pushing down the emotion that would not serve either of them in the end. She was leaving, and hadn't remembered. If she didn't, then maybe that was good. His next step would be to offer himself up as a prospect. It would be unpleasant, but he'd do it to keep Rose safe and get her back to Ballyclare.

The ride through the Cotswolds had been lovely and a distraction for Rose. She'd never been through the small villages and country farms. When they stopped at Chipping Camden, the men roared with laughter as Luce went into a little bakery and came out with a forty-something blonde with a soft figure and cheeky grin. She flipped the sign to close the shop, and hopped on Luce's bike without a backward glance. Twenty-six years had passed, the husband had been disposed of via a divorce lawyer, and she'd been running the bakery on her own ever since. But she hadn't forgotten Luce. Mick was parked next to Jack's bike, and his eyes gleamed with mirth. "Maybe true love does endure."

Rose cocked her head, her helmet off and her hair billowing around her face. "Have you ever…"

"No. Never."

"Twenty years and you've had no one?" Rose asked sadly.

"I had my true love. That doesn't go away so easily. I lost her because I was young and foolish and I wasn't careful. There will never be anyone else." He watched her slide her mother's helmet on her head. "You are so like her. You've got her spirit. I hope you keep finding your memories, Rose, because there were a lot of good ones. She was warm and happy and such a good mother. Protective and attentive. She'd be so proud of you both. When this is done, I'll come to see Kieran." It wasn't a request. "You're adults now, and your grandmother is going to have to deal with it." Rose just stared at him for several seconds. Then she gave a solitary nod.

THE COAST of Wales was breathtaking as they all made camp for the day. Picnic foods and beer cans were brought from the saddle bags and the Welsh chapter showed up to greet them. Rose and Jack walked to a local cafe and purchased a variety of Cornish pasties for themselves and Rose's father. "He doesn't eat enough."

"Neither does his daughter." Jack gave her a chiding look.

Jack walked by a blanket as Luce and Hammer spoke with the local chapter president. Jack heard. "There's an old sea cave that'll do for your purposes. It can get rough, but if they've got the right sort of boat then it'll be perfect."

Jack said casually, "Let's sit and eat these while they're hot." Rose wasn't stupid, she knew why he was doing this. She also wondered if that cell in his pocket was on record. Hammer narrowed his eyes at them as they sat nearby, appearing distracted by their pasties.

Luce said, "I need to know where they are being dispersed. I don't mind them in IRA hands but I don't want them…"

Hammer cut him off, ending the conversation. "We can discuss this later. Let's get another beer."

* * *

As the sun lowered on the horizon, they all boarded their bikes. They had to go back to the bakery to drop off Luce's rider, then return home. Despite some of the questionable company, it had been a good day. Jack felt he'd gotten some key information in a short amount of time. They were smuggling either guns or heroin out of Pembroke in a small patch of uninhabited coastline. A joint venture with the Welsh. He suspected guns. The heroin trade had slowed since a rash of overdoses had happened. Guns or drugs, he'd take it. This could be the key to taking Luce and his club down.

Rose waited for Jack to mount on the bike and start it before she got on. She loved his big Harley. It was a surprise when it didn't start. He tried a few times, then cursed. "It's never done this."

Mick came around Rose and said, "It doesn't sound like it's catching a spark. Let's have a look."

He knelt down and began inspecting the bike when he

froze. "Where did you get these pipes?" His eyes were suspicious. Jackson cursed internally. He'd repainted the bike, but he hadn't changed out the customizations.

Jack said smoothly. "They came with the bike. I bought it off a trader site."

"These are unique. I know because I designed them."

Rose's face blanched. She knew who had owned this bike before. They were separated from the rest of the group, but this whole conversation was scaring her. Her dad might figure out why Jack was here, even though he wouldn't know who he was.

Her father stood up abruptly. "You'll have to tow it to a local shop. Rose can ride back with me."

"Da, I'll just…"

"We have things to discuss, and I don't have my tools or spare parts with me. It's likely a bad spark plug. Just come back with me. He's a big boy, and he can take care of this himself." He leaned in toward Jack. "And then you and I have some things to discuss."

ROSE CHECKED her calls when they pulled over at the bakery. Granny had left a voicemail, hysterics peppering her normally calm tone. Rose screamed with joy. "Oh my God," she choked on a sob. "They found a donor, Da. Kieran has a donor!"

Rose didn't stop smiling all the way back to London. They'd decided not to open the club, or church, as the members called it. They'd let this day settle in their bones. A rare treat, reminiscent of days gone by. Rose checked her texts. Jack had sent two sentences. *My bike was sabotaged. Get the hell out of there.*

Rose snapped. The club was empty except for herself, her

father, and Luce who was in his office. "Did you mess about with his bike so he couldn't come back with us?"

Her father's face flashed with irritation. "What the hell are you on about? I would never disable someone's bike. It's dangerous and stupid. Why do you..." Then he looked at her phone. His face paled. "You need to go home. Now. I don't know who did it, but you need to leave."

The voice was cool behind them. "I did it. I don't trust him. Something stinks about this whole situation." They turned to find Hammer standing in the doorway. Then Luce came into the room.

Luce yelled, "What the hell, Hammer? Put that fecking gun away!" He stood between them and Hammer.

Hammer bristled. "You don't think it's suspicious that he gets grabbed, and right after that we have two new groupies showing up to the club every day? I don't know who the fuck Jackknife is, but he's a novice at best on that bike. And she's got no business here. Why is she still here? Something stinks, and you need to pull your head out of your ass. Obviously Mick gave the feds something and she's helping him."

Mick snapped at him, "Bullshit. You're a paranoid piece of shit. Always have been." Rose grabbed her father's arm, urging him to be quiet. Hammer gave her a once over, and she felt dirty from it.

"Scared, are we, little Rosie? That young buck of yours isn't here to protect you?"

Ice shot up Rose's spine as the men started arguing. Luce demanding the gun, Mick threatening to gut him alive for talking to his daughter like that. But Rose was in the past.

Rose couldn't understand why her mother was so upset. She was packing a baby bag and overnight clothes. Then she heard the motorcycle. "Mammy, is it Da?"

Her mother looked out the window. "No, it's not your da. Rose, darlin', I need you to get in the cupboard." She liked this game, but it didn't feel like fun right now. "Don't come out no matter what you hear." She heard the front door swing open just as her mother closed the door. "I didn't invite you in. You need to leave."

"I don't think I will. We need to talk, Annalise, about what you walked in on." Rose thought she knew the voice. She didn't like Hammer. He was creepy.

"You mean the RPGs you're selling to the Iraqis instead of the Irish? Does Luce know? I never understood the criminal shite you all were into, but you can't sell those guns in the Middle East. For God's sake. Do you know how many innocent people are being killed over there? You shouldn't even be selling them to the feckin' IRA!"

"You don't know shit about this, and you need to keep your fucking hole shut."

Rose was scared. She could hear her brother crying in the nursery, but her mother told her to hide no matter what. Her mother's voice was strained. She was scared too. "I will. I'll keep my mouth shut, Hammer, I swear it. I won't even tell Mick. I just need you to leave. The baby is upset."

"Where's little Rose?" His voice wasn't nice. Rose started to shake as she squatted in that little cupboard.

"She decided to go with her da. They'll be home soon."

But he ignored her. "I don't think so."

Her mother gasped, "Keep your hands off me! Get out of my house!"

"That young buck of yours isn't here, is he? He's in Surrey for the weekend."

The struggle was fast, Rose looked through the vented grate in the metal cabinet and watched in frozen horror. Hammer's hands around her mother's neck. "You will talk, because that's what little bitches like you do. So unfortunately this is where we part ways. But not before I get a little taste of what Mick's been getting. You were always trouble. Luce pining after you like a lovesick boy, Mick thinking you were too good for us and refusing to prospect.

You've been a thorn in my side and it ends today." Her mother choked, trying to grab his hand away as he kissed her hard. He started to pull at her clothes with the other hand. *"If you scream, I'll kill your son. I don't give a shit if he's a baby. The less Tierneys the better."*

She pleaded, *"Please, Hammer. Don't do this. I'm pregnant."*

Jack creeped through the back entrance, not daring to announce his presence. He just hoped to God Nigel's team got here in time. He was outgunned, given the fact that Luce and Hammer were undoubtedly packing and Mick probably wasn't.

Rose started shaking, her face so pale that she looked like she'd seen a ghost. Mick looked at her face and saw the horror. Old horror. He knew her memories were coming back. Something had triggered it. She was looking at either Luce or Hammer. "What is it, Rose? Jesus, what are you seeing?"

Luce turned around and saw her face, then looked at Hammer. "What is going on?" Hammer cocked his head.

Rose's face cleared. She cleared her throat. "She said, *Keep your hands off me! Get out of my house!* And you said, *That young buck of yours isn't here, is he?* I was hidden in the cupboard. I remember." Her voice growled, the pain and the fury roaring in her ears.

Luce said, "Remember what? What is she talking about?" He looked at Mick whose face was filled with unholy rage.

"She hid me. She heard something about a gun deal and you followed her back to the house."

Hammer raised the gun to her. "Best learn from her mistakes and keep your hole shut."

"You tried to rape her. You told her if she screamed, you'd kill Kieran. She begged you. She told you she was pregnant. You fucking animal! You choked her, tied her up. Then you called another biker and you took her away."

The bastard shrugged, "Well, it worked. I'll give her that much. Pregnant women never did it for me."

Luce's face was a sheet of gray. He turned to Hammer and then the gun was on him. Hammer said, "You were getting soft because of that little bitch. You wanted her, and it was killing you. She had a big mouth. I did you a favor. My mistake was not taking Mick out as well. We've made hundreds of thousands of pounds in trade since then. Ah, ah, ah. Leave that gun in your pant leg right where it is, brother."

Rose said, "He was selling guns to the Iraqis during and after the Gulf conflict, instead of to the IRA."

"I told you to shut the fuck up!" Hammer boomed.

"You sold guns to the radicals while my cousin was buried in a Veteran's cemetery?" Luce's face was murderous.

Hammer gave another arrogant shrug. "They paid well, Luce. You never got your hands dirty. Your conscience is clean. That's how this works. Me doing the dirty work, you up on your throne. But these two need to go away. All you need to do is go back in your office or jump on that bike and ride away. I will handle things like I've always done."

"You are a fucking lunatic. I never wanted you as my second, but Mick didn't want any part of it. I should have trusted my instincts when I caught you choking one of my whores. Ye killed Annalise, and there is no place ye can hide from me."

"Fuck you, Luce." Mick growled. "He will die at my hand."

Hammer smiled wickedly. "Too bad you're too much of a pussy to carry a gun." He turned the gun back to Mick just as Jack burst into the room.

Jack said, "Drop that gun or I will put a bullet in your head."

Rose choked on her fear. Jack looked like an avenging angel.

Hammer's laugh made the hair stand up on her arms.

"Fuck me, well played Jackknife. I knew something wasn't right about you. I'm not going to jail, so I guess I'll break some hearts before I go to hell."

Mick jumped in front of his daughter just as Luce screamed and shielded him. The bullet pierced Luce's chest as the other bullet went through the back of Hammer's skull. Then it was chaos. The MI5 entry team burst through the front and side doors, ordering everyone on the ground. Rose ignored them, crawling to Luce as her father was draped over him.

"Get an ambulance!" Rose screamed. Luce coughed, blood coming out of his mouth. Rose was pulling his shirt open, pressing her hand to the arterial bleed. "Oh, God. No! Please, Luce!" she heard the hysteria in her voice. An officer was on the radio calling for an ambulance.

Luce looked at her face, smiling as he struggled to breathe. "I've lived long enough. Prison doesn't appeal to me either, I'm afraid." Then he looked at Mick. "I'm sorry, brother." His eyes welled with tears. "I loved her too. Our beautiful Annalise."

Mick was sobbing. "Why the fuck did you do that, Luce?"

"Because you were always the best of us, and you're needed here, brother. This is the only good thing I've ever done. Let me have it." He coughed, then smiled. "Today was a good day. Like old times," he said weakly. Rose's heart broke because he sounded younger. "And I even got a kiss from a pretty, fair haired lass. It's a good day to go." Mick put his forehead to his old friend's and wept, letting out a heart-wrenching scream.

Luce reached for Rose's hand, stopping her efforts to aid him. "Take me home, Rosie. I want to go home." Then he was gone. The armed men pulled her father off his knees, hand-cuffing him. Rose started CPR, but the blood just spurted from his chest, running between her fingers. When the ambulance came, she finally let go in a heap of bone-crushing despair.

She met her father's eyes. For the second time in his life, he was ruined. She'd known in the moment she'd said it that he hadn't known her mother was pregnant. Now he'd lost his best friend as well.

JACK SAID SOFTLY, "I talked to Nigel. They don't have anything on your father, and I'm not going to lose sleep over that dead biker twenty years ago. His confession will not make it into my report. He'll be released in a few hours. He's telling them everything he knows about the drugs and guns, just so you know. He stayed loyal for Luce. They were close. But he's done with the club. They'll never know he gave us the information. We plan to say Hammer was the informant. No one from that club will ever know what happened in that room. With Mick's help, maybe they can get some of the drugs and guns off the street."

Rose said, "I hope so. Louie would be proud. This was all for him, after all. Right?"

"It started out that way, but no. I did this for you and for Kieran and Annalise. She was a brave woman. She kept you safe. I am so sorry that you remembered her murder."

"I'm not. I'm glad I remembered. For her and for us." She swallowed hard. "It's time for me to go home, Jack. I'll see that Luce is buried with his sister." She got a curious look on her face. "He wasn't a good man, but I can't bring myself to hate him."

"That's the thing about devils, Rose. They're good at temptation and deceit. But you're right, there was some good in him. He saved your father and you." He shuddered at the thought. Then he took her hand, his chest aching. "I wish…"

"No wishing, Jack. No regrets. This was never going to work long-term. You and I are too different. There's no place for me here." She nodded at the bureau by the door. "If you'd kindly take that envelope back to your mother? She never needed to pay me to go back home."

JACK CAME into the flat in the middle of the night, feeling mortally wounded. He was surprised to see Amelia awake in the kitchen. She was eating a very large steak and spuds. He couldn't tell Amelia about today. She didn't know about his other life. He also wouldn't tell her about their mother. She had enough on her plate. Speaking of plates, he shook his head at the late night feast."This is new. Having a late dinner?"

"No, I had a steak and kidney pie for dinner and a treacle tart for my pudding," she said with a smile.

Jack laughed. "I know the doctor told you to indulge, but a steak in the middle of the night?"

"I need to get my iron levels up. Between the supplements and my diet, it won't take long. And I have to gain 13 pounds in six weeks."

He crinkled his brow. "That's a very specific goal. I'm glad you're taking this seriously, but why the urgency?" He was starting to get worried. "Are you sick, Amelia? Is something else wrong?"

"No, Jack. I'm okay. I just need to be one hundred and ten pounds and not anemic in six weeks."

"Amelia, love, you're scaring me. What happens in six weeks?"

She steeled her spine and answered. "In six weeks, they harvest my bone marrow."

$\mathcal{J}$ack gathered the ashes from the crematorium and signed the paperwork. It had been a week since Luce died. Nigel was waiting for him in the car. "You didn't need to do this," Nigel said. "One of those bloody bikers would have done it. They're a loyal lot, for all that."

"He died protecting Rose. He was a dodgy bastard, to say the least, but he's not the one who laced that heroin with fentanyl. The fatal dose of heroin hitting the streets was Hammer's doing. And Luce didn't put that needle in my brother's arm. Louie did that on his own."

"It seems you've gained some perspective. Will you give the remains to Mr. Tierney?"

"Yes, he's headed across the water tomorrow. They'll inter the ashes in his sister's grave. Then they'll visit Annalise's grave. She's buried in the same cemetery outside of Belfast."

"How touching," he said dryly. "Now, the shrink has cleared you for duty. I may not have liked some of your choices, but full marks for the end result. And don't lose any sleep over that bastard you put in the ground." He patted Jack on the back, lecture over. "Are you ready to get a fucking haircut and get back in your Armani suits?" Jack just nodded absently. Nigel sighed. "Christ, you are a hopeless sap. Maybe this next assignment will cheer you up."

He handed Jack the file and he thumbed through it. Then he rifled through the papers again urgently. "This is in Belfast."

"Is it? Well, isn't that a coincidence? Apparently there's suspicion of financial espionage. Russians, they think."

Jack's grin almost cracked his face. "Christ, you are a hopeless sap," he jibed, throwing Nigel's words back at him.

"You can thank Katherine. She advised me, like I was an idiot, that Northern Ireland was part of the UK and within our jurisdiction. Then she grabbed this case off the hot-fill sheet and demanded I assign you. You know how she is. All those romance novels. There would be no living with her if I said no."

"You are a proper bastard some days, Nigel, but I owe you for this one."

"Just go pack your things. You'll need to be gone long term. This isn't going to be easy, but I do think you are ready. After we intercepted that load of guns off the coast of Pembroke, my boss is in the mood to grant me a favor. Don't worry about Amelia. We'll watch the houses."

Jack smiled, stupidly happy. "No worries on that account. Amelia comes with me. She has her own business in Belfast."

ROSE STARED out the window of their kitchen, thinking about the night Jack had kissed her behind the shed. The tears seemed endless in the nighttime, but she kept them contained during the day. "You should call him. I liked him," her granny's voice said behind her.

"You don't understand, Gran. We are too different. You don't know everything."

"I know you found your father. I know that in some way Jack helped you through that. He's a good sort, as is Amelia. And by the looks of that suit he was wearing, he can pay his rent."

She smiled at that. If Gran only knew. She looked up as she saw a car come into the driveway. Another came in behind it. A Jaguar and a Jeep. Jack climbed out, looking too good to be legal, and her heart jumped in her throat. Then Amelia came out of the Jeep waving like a lunatic. "I take that back. He looks like he could buy the whole building. Nice car."

Kieran came through the kitchen door, pale and groggy from a week of chemotherapy. "Nice car. Is that…" Rose shot out the front door, but then stopped before she got to them. Maybe he had bad news. But then he wouldn't have brought Amelia, would he? She approached slowly.

Jack splayed out his hands, his heart in his eyes. Hot tears pricked her eyes. "This is the real me, love. No leather, four wheels, but it's all yours if you'll have me. I've just been assigned a permanent position in our Belfast office. It turns out Nigel, the Smug English Bastard, is a bit of a romantic." Rose closed the distance in a flash, legs around his waist, kissing him all over his face. "I'll take that as a yes?" He laughed. She put her face in his neck and smelled the masculine scent of him. He pulled her tight. "I couldn't do it. I couldn't stay away. I tried, but I love you, Rose. I love you most desperately."

She squeezed harder, whispering in his neck, "I love you, too."

"Then you'll come house hunting with us." Not a question. "Something big enough to expand the family, but warm like this place." He smiled at Keirsty.

That got Rose's attention. "Expand? Oh! I'm not pregnant, Jack!" she assured him. "Were ye worried, then?"

"No, actually I may have been hoping a little." He was blushing. Jesus, Nigel was right. He was a sap, but he'd come here for one reason. "I suppose we should get married first, but I'd like a family. I mean, if that's what you want. I poached Judith from my mother's staff. She'll be a great help. As will you, Keirsty. We'll be a big, messy, happy family."

Rose's tears overflowed. He said softly, "You could do with some happy years, Rose, and you're going to get them. All of you." He gave a conspiratorial glance toward his sister, and he noticed she was fighting her own tears. "We're your happy ending, my beautiful, wild, Irish Rose."

Made in United States
North Haven, CT
25 January 2022

15246583R00104